Ecstasy Romance ®

"TELL ME WHO YOU ARE, NIALL. DON'T MAKE A FOOL OF ME."

He arched his back, rising from her to prop himself on stiffened arms. "What . . . are . . . you . . . saying?"

She should have told him. Immediately told him all she'd discovered, but she wanted the truth from him, freely given.

"What I could tell you would hurt," he said in a voice grown scratchy and rough. "Believe me. Don't ask questions, Sara. Enjoy what we have. What little we can have of this, for only three short weeks."

Three weeks. Love for three weeks? She planted her fists against his chest to push him away.

"Then I don't want you!" she cried. She was lying, of course, and close to tears.

"Okay," he said curtly. "Good luck sleeping, Miss MacFarland. Ms. MacFarland, rather. If you change your mind . . . just whistle."

CANDLELIGHT ECSTACY ROMANCES ®

SECRETS FOR SHARING

Carol Norris

A CANDLELIGHT ECSTASY ROMANCE ®

Published by
Dell Publishing Co., Inc.
1 Dag Hammarskjold Plaza
New York, New York 10017

ISBN: 0–440–17614–X

Printed in the United States of America
First printing—June 1984

For all my Canadian friends—May, especially.

*And for Humboldters who write, fish, and fly—
and have been very patient.*

To Our Readers:

We have been delighted with your enthusiastic response to Candlelight Ecstasy Romances®, and we thank you for the interest you have shown in this exciting series.

In the upcoming months we will continue to present the distinctive sensuous love stories you have come to expect only from Ecstasy. We look forward to bringing you many more books from your favorite authors and also the very finest work from new authors of contemporary romantic fiction.

As always, we are striving to present the unique, absorbing love stories that you enjoy most—books that are more than ordinary romance.

Your suggestions and comments are always welcome. Please write to us at the address below.

Sincerely,

The Editors
Candlelight Romances
1 Dag Hammarskjold Plaza
New York, New York 10017

CHAPTER ONE

Sara MacFarland was bone-weary. She had flown for seventeen hours on four different aircraft to reach this wild valley in British Columbia. Though back home in Kentucky it was almost midnight, here the sun was still up. Still above the mountains at eight thirty in the evening! The last leg of her long journey consisted of a ride into the valley on the single-engine mail plane that visited here only twice a week. Now safe in the valley, she ought immediately to go to the little Canadian town's sole hotel and put herself to bed. She needed sleep badly.

Something about this town seemed very peculiar, however. The fact began to sink into her groggy mind that Chilto looked eerily deserted. How intriguing. Like the site for a disaster movie. On this evergreen-scented, quiet, lovely August evening, where could all its citizens be?

The pilot could stay only long enough to stash the incoming mail in the post office section of the town's tradestore, and then pick up the outgoing mail. Dusk would soon fall. Before he departed for civilization again, however, he suggested they deposit Sara's suitcases and

11

her trunks of research supplies in the store overnight so that she'd have to carry only one small case. She certainly didn't feel eager to lug much more, since she'd had no sleep for the past two nights. The journey to Canada had taken a tremendously long time. She was too tired even to be hungry.

The town café was obviously closed; it was good that she had no appetite. Each airline that helped transport her here had dutifully served her a big meal. She had breakfast as she flew over Kentucky, followed by lunch over Colorado, and dinner over California—with cocktails and coffee in between.

The coffee had kept her awake to gaze down from the plane windows at the whole width of the United States. Then heading north along the West Coast, she had flown right past Mt. St. Helens volcano in Washington's Cascade Range. Late in the afternoon she finally reached Canada, her own Canada, which she had idealized for so many years.

"I am a Canadian," she said to herself, liking the sound of her words.

As she said good-bye to the helpful mail pilot, she glimpsed through the door of the store a black-haired man striding down the unpaved road. His limbs looked strong and supple. She couldn't see enough of his face to guess his age. His brown and green plaid shirt and close-fitting faded jeans matched the forest setting. One of the local lumberjacks? His high cheekbones under the tanned skin, and the tall, broad-shouldered physique made her think he might claim some Indian ancestry.

Because he hadn't seen her standing in the front doorway of the store, she decided not to call attention to herself. She didn't need any help. Besides, he was almost too good-looking; she wasn't in Canada for a fling or even a small infatuation. Far from it.

12

"You're here for two purposes," she reminded herself patiently. "First, to make a small contribution to medical science. Second, to prove some colleagues wrong. Some fellows back in Kentucky, to be exact, who told her right to her face that she'd never complete her British Columbia project. Ruefully she recalled how all five of them laughed at her angry expression and balled fists.

"Why can't I succeed?" she'd demanded. "I've got just about the same training and experience as many of you. Why not?"

"Because you're small and fragile and far too feminine to be up in the north woods all by yourself," one had had the nerve to respond.

So furious that she didn't even remember which man said it, she'd stormed out of the lab, packed her bags, and headed to Canada. She still got angry remembering their sneers. It wasn't her small size that bothered them. They would have made the same cracks if she had been tall, or middle-aged, or plain, or even brilliant. No matter what a woman looked like, she wasn't really welcome in their research laboratory. Unless, of course, she kept busy washing their test tubes or typing their reports.

Sara stepped out onto the narrow gravel sidewalk as the pilot locked the door of the tradestore behind her. He was in a hurry to get back to the airstrip and fly home before night fell. The stranger she'd glimpsed in this seemingly deserted town had already vanished, so Sara found herself completely alone; not one other soul had appeared.

In the display window of the country store a handwritten announcement caught her eye. It was pasted on the glass and said INDIAN DANCES, AUGUST 9, 8 P.M.

She consulted her watch to assure herself that it was August 9. It was also past 8 P.M., so the attraction of these "Indian Dances" probably explained the emptiness of the

13

town. Everyone was at the dances, but where were they being held?

She stared at the straggling row of frame buildings on the graveled roadway—bank, bakery, café. Still no sign of life, but when she listened carefully she could pick up faint strains of music—music wafting across the wide river. The mail plane, bringing her into the valley, had followed that river from the site of its origins—a series of dramatic waterfalls cascading down from a high inland plateau. The river surged, violently foaming, through this long valley to empty into the Pacific Ocean. The town of Chilto lay at the head of a fjord slicing 100 miles into the coast of British Columbia. There was no way to get there except by plane or mule train or by coastal ship. No road fit for automobiles, the mail pilot told her, could be built over such precipices through such rugged terrain.

In this wilderness, Sara realized, she would be completely anonymous. No one in British Columbia knew she was coming except one fisheries official who made a long-distance telephone call to Kentucky to tell her when the salmon run began. No one was here to greet her, to welcome her to Canada, to make her feel at home. On the other hand, no one would be likely to interfere with her work—no one would tell her that she was too small or too slight for the research project that now faced her. And no one could say she was too young. She wasn't, not at twenty-seven, but she knew she looked half a dozen years younger. The mop of short brown curls didn't help, nor did the childishly short nose and large gray-green eyes.

As Sara headed in the direction of the music—music now mixed with laughter and applause which she could clearly hear, she did not hurry. She sauntered along, swinging her overnight bag, breathing deeply of the odor of the spruces and fir trees as she admired her dazzling surroundings.

14

Dark, spiky, evergreen-covered slopes rose almost vertically to wall in this narrow valley. Against their green darkness, brilliant pink fireweed glowed at the rushing river's edge. Up the valley eastward, white peaks of gigantic, snowy mountains were still brightly sunlit. An ancient glacier hung from the open maw of the highest peak. Sara relished the glorious display of untouched nature. All the colors seemed incredibly vivid, like those in nature paintings sold in dime stores. The mountains' deep snow pack and the glacier all summer had fed melt-water into the river that had carved this valley, turning its waters surprisingly pale. Pale but surely pure enough to drink.

That river—plus an unexpected man-made barrier to her progress—now lay before her, and brought Sara to an anxious halt.

She was neither a weakling nor a coward. She'd grown up as the sole sister of several boisterous brothers, and her biological field work required miles of hiking as well as occasional rock climbing and the fording of wide rivers on slippery stones. What discouraged her today was the means by which she'd have to cross this particular river that cut her off from the mysterious music. Sara called up a little extra courage. For the first time in her life she'd have to step out upon a suspension bridge, a flimsy spiderweb made of wires and boards. The railing of this literally "swinging" bridge was no higher than her waist. Crossing it would be like walking a tightrope over the murderously violent river.

When she put her weight upon it, the bridge bucked and swayed. Suddenly, more weight was added—a little child materialized out of nowhere and came pelting across the bridge, shoving past Sara in his haste. Sara dropped to a crouch, fingers clutching the wires of the bridge; she stared down at the foaming, icy green water only inches below the soles of her boots.

Somehow she managed to creep the rest of the way across, following that running child who had shown no more concern than a tiny spider dashing along a filament.

Sara stopped gulping air, forced herself to smile wryly, and mentally chalked up yet another adventure for today. What a day! One thing more to write home about—home to relatives and friends back in Kentucky. Her folks had given her a new camera for the trip—a camera which she kept tucked inside her overnight case to avoid being labeled "tourist." Good friends in Lexington had thrown two going-away parties for her; it was those celebrations that cost her the last two nights of sleep. Every man she ever dated, it seemed, came to one or both parties to wish her bon voyage and to warn her about marauding Canadian moose, grizzly bears, and wolves . . . four-legged and two-legged varieties, both.

Her supercilious male colleagues at the institute certainly had lectured her—not on the topic of wild animals, but about the supposed weaknesses of women. They expected her to cop out, drop out, and come dragging home dripping wet and humiliated. No way! She'd just crossed her first swaying suspension bridge, and soon she would be wrestling Pacific salmon, to learn why they grew ancient in only a few weeks. Any answers to that question would give physicians more weapons against aging in human beings.

Across the turbulent river Sara found herself entering another small town. She was drawing nearer to the source of the music. Sounds poured through the open double doors of a community hall set just inside a split-rail fence. The building was obviously crowded, for it was practically shivering on its foundations.

"Indian dances?" Now she'd see for herself what that term meant.

In the doorway Sara paused. She gazed at the backs of

hundreds of men, women, and children, all seated facing away from her toward a stage. There were blond heads and black, and every shade in between. Immediately Sara felt more at ease. This was not a dance in the sense of a disco or a square dance. It was some sort of performance, intriguing enough to empty whole towns this Friday night. She glimpsed a row of dark-haired women leaving the stage amidst earnest applause and soft murmurs from the crowd. Sara searched the long rows of backless benches for space to sit down and watch.

Suddenly a diminutive old woman wearing jeans and a denim jacket stepped up beside Sara and seized her arm in a determined grip. Startled, Sara barely kept from wrenching her arm away, but the big smile on the stranger's rosy, wrinkled face prevented her from demanding her freedom. The old woman was practically hugging her.

Suddenly the woman announced in a rasping quaver, "So here you are, Sara MacFarland! And am I the first to get hold of you? Splendid, lass! Let's find you a seat right up front!"

"I'd rather sit in back, if you don't mind," Sara responded. Then, less politely she asked, "How on earth do you know my name?"

"We have our ways," the old woman said, dramatically rolling faded blue eyes. "Come. First row, front and center, is the spot for a newcomer, a real woman scientist!" she stated, emphasizing the last two words.

Sara was too astonished to ask if anyone ever says "man scientist." This was no time or place to squabble over women's rights. Her determined little guide was energetically hauling her down the center aisle toward the stage. Sara offered no resistance, fearing that would cause even more of a stir in the crowd. Everyone was already turning to stare. "Good ole Ruth!" someone remarked, and Sara heard several other echoes of that sentiment.

17

"I'm Ruth Bell," the woman told Sara. "Call me Ruth. Here we are. Shove over a bit there, Andy. Sit down, Sara. You must be worn out by all that traveling. All the way from Ken-tucky," she chuckled.

Front row was indeed where Sara landed. In the front row, dead center, right underneath the stage. Ruth hollowed out space for them both.

"I . . . look, how do you know so much about me?" Sara asked. "What's going on here anyway?"

Then Sara's attention was drawn to the stage. The next act, dance, or whatever seemed now to be beginning.

Sara stared in amazement. From behind the folds of dusty red curtains appeared a masked dancer. Her eyes opened wide because the man had on almost nothing at all. His head was covered by a mask carved into the beak of a fearsome hawk, and for clothing he wore only a pair of dark bathing trunks.

Sara gasped as the dancer in the mask moved with ease under that carved wooden head resting upon his broad shoulders. His beautifully constructed body shone an even golden color. He began a twisting, stamping dance, this man as smooth as an animated wood carving. To the rhythm of invisible drums he clashed two sticks together in front of his body—his absolutely magnificent male body.

Ruth Bell had obtained a mimeographed piece of paper from the person seated on the other side of her, and shoved the paper into Sara's hands. "Look," she said.

Sara looked where Ruth was pointing. She caught the words Rain Dancer. The dancer's name was Elmer Snagg.

Elmer Snagg? Well, there goes half his charisma!

Poor guy! thought Sara. *With a name like that, he surely deserves to have a body to make men envious and women sit up and take note—even exhausted women scientists.*

18

Oddly, she felt much less tired now. The dancer took her mind off herself.

One thing for sure. Sara did *not* want to see any rain dancer's dance bring rain. She loved the valley's sunny, glorious, 75-degree climate; she'd need lots more of this cloudless August weather to accomplish her work. No rain!

But that didn't mean she couldn't relish watching this particular rain dancer, did it?

Sara stared transfixed at the dancer. No longer did her eyes feel tired. She parted her lips and found herself gripping the front edge of the bench. When Ruth Bell nudged her, Sara ignored the interruption, but didn't miss the teasing look in the old woman's sideways glance.

The rain dancer's bare feet kept beat with a rainlike pattering of drums from behind the curtains. He sharply struck his polished sticks together while he turned his fierce mask from side to side. Sara didn't think he could see anything through the eyeholes that pierced such thick wood. He must be dancing blind.

Everyone had fallen silent, even the young children. This dance was not in any sense comical; it was totally serious, completely masculine. He turned and bent, his shapely arms outstretched, his muscular legs braced, flexing, bracing, flexing. His muscles stood up in ridges as he swooped, birdlike. He beseeched the spirits for rain with the supple tiltings and swirlings of his narrow-waisted bronze torso. He did not speak or chant, but Sara could hear his breath panting—hissing inside the echo chamber of the hollow mask.

The mask was painted a gaudy red and black and glared down at her from above a chest and abdomen that looked as hard as leather. Sara grew so alert, she could coolly examine her own emotions. Though she certainly didn't welcome any emotional involvement with anyone up here in British Columbia, she could still look, couldn't she? Look but don't touch. She couldn't even plan to go out in the evenings, because her evenings would be taken up with laboratory analyses.

She continued, however, to gaze up at this epitome of male perfection. To be so firm-muscled, he was probably very young, barely out of his teens. She felt little interest in meeting the bronzed dancer, or even in catching a glimpse of the face behind the frighteningly ferocious mask. Why make of the magnificent rain dancer a mundane, imperfect human being? He probably raced a motorcycle, smoked pot, and cursed. Let him remain anonymous, as anonymous as she had planned to be before Ruth broke the spell. She had called her by name and knew her profession too. What else did Ruth Bell know?

Boy, don't I sound paranoid! she teased herself, admitting that the woman's cheerful warmth felt rather comforting, now that she'd weathered the first shock.

"Sit back and enjoy yourself, Sara," she muttered to herself between her teeth. She'd watch this dancer the way a man might watch a gorgeous woman dance.

Oddly intriguing, tonight, to feel somewhat the way a man must feel, some man in a bar where semi-nude women dance on tables with their faces hidden in layers of cigar and cigarette smoke. There was no smoke in this high-ceilinged hall, and Sara became gradually aware of the acceleration of her pulse and a growing warmth spreading through her body. Intriguing. Rather pleasant sensations, in fact. *I must be really tired,* she told herself.

The dancer's ever-moving body shone with perspiration now; he glittered in the warm, crowded room. Reds and golds from the western sky were striping the wall opposite the tall, dusty windows. Other walls featured brightly painted murals of totemic animals.

"Ever seen dancing like that?" asked Ruth Bell.

Sara shook her head no.

"Dunno who this fellow Snagg is, but he's a looker, isn't he, lass?" the old woman remarked. "The people around here don't get soft and flabby, sittin' on their tails all day. Present company excepted."

Sara didn't comment, because she was distracted by the sudden end of the dance and the departure of the rain dancer from the stage. He went behind the curtains, and she joined in the applause. *Hurrah for you, Elmer, handsome Elmer Snagg, who must fell giant trees, or haul salmon in heavy nets, to build a body like that.* The audience was still clapping and stamping booted, bare, or moccasined feet on the springy footboards.

Ruth jostled Sara and pointed to the next dance on the program. Dance number eight was called "How-How Birds." The how-hows themselves came careening out from behind the curtain just then. They were boys wearing bark-cloth cloaks and masks with yard-long green and red beaks. Sara felt intrigued by these human birds, but the rain dancer still obsessed her. She missed him. It was foolish, but harmlessly foolish if she ignored her disturbingly strong erotic response to the man. She must try to conceal her feelings from Ruth, who was studying her with an amused smile on her unpainted lips.

Sara's own lips were by now also unpainted. She'd given up repairing her makeup about the time she boarded the mail plane. No need for cosmetics and designer clothes in the Chilto Valley, especially since her stay would be so short. In only a month she'd be headed home, her precious research data in hand. A private foundation financed most of her trip, and winning a grant from them meant long months spent writing her project proposal, gathering recommendations, and trying to sound modest while describing every ability she possessed. Too bad she had to spend so much needed energy feeling defensive. But the men's expectation—or hope—that she'd do a rotten, half-baked "woman's" job increased her desire to exceed all expectations—her own and everyone else's.

Who came up with the saying "A woman needs a man like a fish needs a bicycle"?

Probably true. True at least for the duration of her Canadian summer.

CHAPTER TWO

Niall Whitethorne, having exited from the stage, walked into a curtained cubicle before he freed his head of the stifling mask he had worn during the rain dance. He winced at reddened lacerations that the mask's lower edge had rubbed into his bare flesh. Splinters were ground into his collarbones, and he'd have to apply antiseptic to the wounds.

He had taken Elmer Snagg's place when that youngster had gotten an acute case of stage fright and refused to dance half naked in front of a large audience that included his parents and all four grandparents. The moment Niall walked in the door of the community hall, Elmer had snagged him—he winced at his own pun. They'd never met, but the kid was frantic to avoid dancing on stage. Niall, almost without thinking, agreed to substitute as the rain dancer. There was no other man who knew the dance well and could fit into young Elmer's swim trunks.

Niall found the dance was not difficult. He'd danced here as a boy, and it came back naturally. Like driving a car or typing, you never forget the moves. The legs and the arms remember.

Wearing that heavy wooden mask made him feel like some beast of burden weighed down under some farmer's yoke, but for performing the dance he had received one interesting reward—he got the rapt attention of the attractive Yank who'd flown into the valley today with the mail plane. Half an hour ago he'd spotted her standing in the doorway of the tradestore, talking to the pilot, but she had not seen him. He'd kept on walking, headed for the reserve and this dance exhibition.

And then she was suddenly there, seated in the audience, in the very first row in the middle, staring up at him without any attempt to disguise her interest. Hardly blinking, she'd leaned forward, her lips parted—coral lips in a healthy, rosy face. Her hair was a soft mass of curls much thicker than the tinted curls on Ruth Bell's ancient head and much lighter than his own black hair. Ruth sat right beside the Yank, so it was probably Ruth who'd dragged the girl up to the front row. While he danced he'd studied the pretty face and the yellow shirt and vest that she filled out so nicely. He had also noticed the small suitcase stuck between her cowboy boots. She had light eyes, maybe gray.

Ruth Bell must have swooped like a tiny falcon to capture the girl somewhere between the town and the hall. The few days he'd spent back in this valley were sufficient to educate him to Ruth's ways.

Sixteen years had passed since Ruth's husband had grabbed up Green Lodge. Wanting it as his retirement home, he blithely ended its history as a hunting lodge. When he closed off half the rooms in 1967, Niall's mother and father found themselves out of work. The three Whitethornes left Chilto Valley for Prince Rupert, in the north. He'd been fifteen back then, and very bitter about their eviction. His father was philosophical about it. "At least the bears will be happier," he said, "with fewer rich trophy hunters around."

Old Mr. Bell didn't enjoy his giant house for very long. He died, and his widow now kept herself occupied by delving into everyone's life history. Ironically, his own life history was still secret from her. So far.

Tonight she'd ambushed this Yankee newcomer, a girl hardly taller than herself. He'd have to watch out; like many bored widows, Ruth was not only a snoop; she was also a matchmaker.

Shaking his head, Niall went into the washroom backstage, shed the bathing trunks, washed up, and toweled himself dry vigorously. He got back into his jeans and flannel shirt, wincing when the collar settled on the abrasions left from the mask. He combed his hair straight back from his forehead and over the tops of his ears, bending to look into the rusty-framed mirror hanging askew on the wall. The light was fading. Time to get back up the mountain, but Ruth would probably insist on being the last person to leave the hall.

He wrung out the bathing trunks over the sink—Elmer Snagg's trunks. He'd made Elmer promise only one thing: there'd be no announcement about the substitute rain dancer. Let Elmer get the credit or blame, and Niall, absent from this valley for the past sixteen years, would remain anonymous. Fair enough.

Niall left Nuhauk Hall by the back door and walked around the building. To ease the blisters raised by a new pair of boots, he'd yesterday purchased deerskin moccasins scented faintly with woodsmoke. They proved very comfortable, like his plaid flannel shirt and his soft jeans rubbed white along the seams. No more starched white coats for a while. He was tired, burned out. He'd come back to his home looking for peace and solitude, glad that

25

he knew every inch of these forests, and that few who now lived here remembered him. Even fewer would be rude enough to ask questions or even mention his long absence.

After a few days beside the river, his nights spent in a sleeping bag, he'd felt a need for a bit of hard physical labor to loosen up his muscles. Ironically, the leaky roof at Green Lodge provided the only easily available job.

Ruth Bell had shown him around the place as if he were a tourist, and offered his choice of rooms in the cavernous old hunting lodge. Unsuspecting, she gave him the room he'd asked for, the one his parents had once occupied.

From the lodge's lofty perch on the mountainside, he could see halfway to the Pacific Ocean. In Ruth's seaplane he was able to soar even higher, and could practically see the southern tip of Alaska.

As for his little stateside admirer, he'd wager that by now Ruth had persuaded her to join them up at Green Lodge. There wasn't anything he could do about that.

Niall squinted into the red and purple sunset and shook his head. Then he began to walk more quickly, and with purpose.

He did not go down to the harbor to wait beside Ruth's seaplane as he had previously planned. Instead, he climbed the front steps of Nuhauk Hall and entered the building again. He glided quietly down the center aisle and found space on the second row of benches in the center. Not by accident he sat directly behind Ruth Bell and her new young friend with the curly hair and the admiring gaze. He settled down so gingerly and silently that neither woman saw or heard him arrive.

The narrator, a tall woman with a pleasantly cadenced alto voice, was intoning: "Legends say that holding a staff upon your feet will save you from being killed in the night by a how-how. If shot with arrows, they do not die, but are resurrected . . ."

26

The performing how-how birds wore wreaths of twigs above their masks to represent hair. *Hair and teeth on birds must really perplex that Yankee stranger,* mused Niall. A guide was accompanying each how-how to make sure its beak did not take a bite out of some child leaning, enthralled, onto the stage. The little Yankee seemed less enthralled than she'd been when he, the rain dancer, was performing. She looked all about her, pivoting from the waist to her left and right.

Then she tilted her head down close to Ruth's, whispering, "I wish the rain dancer would come back for an encore."

Niall jerked back, flabbergasted. Then he carefully leaned forward again, his elbows on his knees. Ruth Bell's old face had wrinkled into a pixie grin, but the stranger was not yet finished. Then she added, whispering, "He had the most marvelous build I've ever seen!"

Niall's own lips now curled, half in amusement, half in consternation. If Ruth guessed who the rain dancer was, how would she describe the itinerant workman hired to repair her roof? But Ruth didn't say anything about him. He'd fooled that sharp old falcon as well.

When the how-hows left the stage, Niall frowned at the next masked figures bounding onto the platform. This was the final dance, something obviously new since his youth in this valley, because there were no bare legs showing beneath the cloaks worn by these three tall men. Instead, knife-creased trousers were evident, plus the sort of black dress shoes seldom seen in the back country. The three pranced about in an irritating parody of the Indian dances. Suddenly one bird-headed figure whipped out a large hypodermic syringe and began squirting the others with liquid. Another was waving a big aluminum-foil scalpel. Hearing the audience laugh and applaud, Niall suddenly realized who the three men must be.

Ruth was informing her new friend of the same discovery.

"The valley doctors come to make fools of themselves here every year," she whispered loudly. "Contributes to community cohesion."

Niall snorted to himself. Cohesion, indeed! And who was attending the hospital patients in the absence of these fools? Two of the three were city doctors up from Vancouver for the summer. He'd already heard rumors that they spent every free hour fishing. The resident surgeon, the youngest of the three, was barely thirty. As he took off his mask and bowed, he was staring down directly at Ruth's pretty friend.

Niall worried about the hospital, tonight depending entirely on its nursing staff. No critical cases better come in while these three were making a spectacle of themselves in Nuhauk Hall.

Ruth Bell's next comment jostled his thoughts.

"Before the old folks forget their oral traditions, the younger ones must learn to do the dances."

"I see," the girl murmured gravely.

"These used to be rituals of high seriousness. The rain dancer did bring rain, and the thunderbirds dropped lightning bolts from on high."

Her student listened with a sober face while Niall, unseen by either of them, glowered. Who was Ruth Bell, only sixteen years in this valley, to expound on Indian lore? And even worse, to express herself so poetically?

"In the olden days Indians used trapdoors, smokescreens, and speaking-tubes in these ceremonies," Ruth rattled on. "You can borrow my books about it."

The program was over. Old Rasco Burns commenced to blow a tin horn in the ears of people on the left aisle, and the woman narrator was fending off some clown who'd donned a woolen horror mask. The audience started rising and stretching. Children, unleashed, dashed forward to purchase soft drinks and handle the masks being placed on display in a row along the edge of the stage.

Niall lowered his gaze and found himself staring at the trim waist and the pleasant backside of the Yankee girl. These delicacies were set no more than three inches in front of his kneecaps. He took care not to close the distance. The brown denim of her jeans was stretched so tight that the tiny stitches of the midseam showed. She was again sitting tall and twisting to left and right as if searching for someone. Niall dipped his head and cupped a hand over his brow, pretending to study the rumpled program he found on the floor.

"There's a dear little museum in town, but few tourists find this valley," Ruth was raving on. "I know you'll love it here, assuming you survive."

"Survive?" That word startled Niall into lifting his head abruptly. The movement attracted Ruth's attention, and she recognized him.

"Why, I didn't see you when I came in, Niall!" she exclaimed, spinning the girl around to face him. "Sara MacFarland, meet Niall Whitethorne, and vice versa."

So the Yank's name was Sara. She was even better-looking up close than from his perch on stage. Her face was softly rounded, tanned, and on the edges pale with sunbleached down that he'd love to stroke. The upturned nose took years off her age, which he decided must be the mid-twenties when he spotted the laugh lines beside her eyes. Fine. Girls much younger than that have little they can talk about. Sara's eyes were green. Merry eyes, but badly bloodshot.

Niall murmured something in the way of greetings or good wishes, distracted by the intense way Sara kept staring at him. He could actually see his brown eyes and wide

29

mouth reflected in her gaze. He slumped forward to disguise the width of his shoulders. He couldn't have Ruth start shrieking that he, and not Elmer, must have been the half-naked rain dancer.

"Niall's taken on the task of putting shake shingles on my roof," Ruth remarked. "Niall, wouldn't it be jolly if Sara joined us up at the lodge?"

He could easily guess what that remark implied.

"Join you?" the girl innocently echoed.

"You can't think of stopping at that crackerbox of a hotel in town," Ruth exclaimed. "You must spend the month at my place instead. Free of charge. I get lonely, and Mr. Bell left me darned well off financially. The views from Green Lodge are terrific. The old place will just thrill you . . . spitless!"

Sara said nothing. Niall marveled at the serene self-confidence of old age.

"Niall lives up at the lodge too," Ruth went on. "I met and adopted him just a few days ago. The more the merrier, wouldn't you say? When you see all the cozy rooms standing empty in my big house—well, you can take your pick."

The little Yank's lips moved, but no words came. Niall felt blood simmer in his veins at the notion of getting to know this girl, of closing his hands over those delightful curves set before him, and then exploring every detail of her delightful body.

If he could endure Ruth Bell for a while longer, he might revive in Sara MacFarland the feelings she'd so obviously displayed while she watched him dance.

CHAPTER THREE

Sara resisted the urge to stare at the man who'd been seated right behind them. He now was standing up, towering over both Ruth and her. He was definitely the same man she'd seen walking through the town when she first arrived. Had he slipped into the woods, out of sight, and waited until she got ahead of him? Did he follow her here? She certainly had not seen him when she was dragged down to the front row; therefore, he had to come in later than she did. Interesting. She'd had plenty of men follow her around, and need not pay special attention to this one, except that this man lived up at Green Lodge, worked for Ruth Bell, and was striking looking. He said very little, but his soft baritone was pleasant to the ears.

How odd to have felt a momentary obsession with the rain dancer, and now to find herself dwelling upon this man too. Elmer Snagg and Niall Whitethorne—what a contrast in names!

Niall's sleek black hair sparkled with hints of red in the electric lights that had flashed on as dusk fell. His face was neither flat nor broad, nor as dark as those of many people in the hall. His tan was only a shade or two darker than hers, and the sharply defined planes of his face would make a sculptor happy. His deep-set eyes were expressive, and as Ruth rattled on, his lean, very cleanly shaven face kept changing expression.

Niall like the River Nile? His looks—though certainly not his name—did, in fact, seem a trifle Egyptian.

The crowd began edging toward trestle tables along one wall, where wide-mouthed jugs and casserole dishes were magically appearing. Ruth started beckoning to people, shouting greetings in her raspy voice and pointing at Sara. The big room rocked with the hubbub, from the plank flooring to the exposed ceiling beams.

"My Yankee," Ruth called Sara.

Sara glanced over at Niall, found him staring boldly at her, and muttered so only she herself could hear: "I'm a Yankee Canadian or a Canadian Yankee then."

Men and women were popping out of the crowd to shake Ruth's hand—both her hands. Indians and Caucasians slapped the tiny woman on the back, nearly capsizing her. Sara, who definitely did not wish to spend an entire month lodging with the valley gossip or any ornery old witch, took careful note. Judging by the number of Ruth's friends, however, and the fondness with which they greeted the old woman, Sara began to be convinced of the wisdom of staying at the lodge. It would be far less lonely than hotel life . . . but would Niall prove something of a problem?

"How old are you, Sara?" Ruth suddenly demanded, in the midst of introducing her to numerous people whose names Sara knew she'd never be able to remember.

"I'm—" But Ruth was off on a tangent.

"How old you think I am?" Ruth demanded, fists on her hips. "Just guess!"

"Uh . . . about seven—I mean sixty-five?" Sara ventured.

"Off by twenty years!" she exulted. "I'm going on eighty-five! How's about that?" She hitched up her jeans. "And you?"

"Twenty-seven," said Sara, noticing that Niall cocked a brow as if bemused by her prompt frankness.

"You don't look your age anymore'n I look *my* age. Does she, Niall? You hear what this little slip of a thing is planning on doing, Niall? All month long?"

"I can't imagine," said Niall Whitethorne.

"Studying live salmon, that's what."

"How did you know?" Sara demanded. "I didn't meet a single soul in town; you were the first person I spoke to—"

"You talked to Mark Fawcett, who flew you in, and he's got a radio. Didn't you notice that?"

"Oh, brother!"

Her pilot had indeed spent a lot of time speaking into his tiny microphone, his speech inaudible over the noise of the plane's engine. So he'd been busy alerting the whole valley to her arrival! *Gee thanks, fella,* she thought ruefully.

Niall found his voice at last. "Salmon streams in spawning season are full of grizzlies," he said. "Bears. Anyone tell you about them?"

His brow was like a thundercloud over the dark, intent eyes studying her. Sara felt shivers course down her back, which had nothing to do with grizzlies. Niall himself was disturbing enough.

"Well, I hope there's room enough in the streams and river for all of us," she said cheerfully. "For me and the salmon and the bears."

His glare darkened, and then turned into a wry grin.

"Come see the masks," he said in his soft deep voice.

Sara thought she detected a different intonation, as if he now were teasing. Why? The masks were certainly interesting objects.

Sara lifted a how-how mask from the edge of the stage and found it surprisingly heavy. She ran a fingertip into the eyehole of the rain dancer's fierce red and black mask, guessing that the wearer might have been able to see after all. Niall Whitethorne continued to stand close behind her. Heat radiated from his body, as if he had a fever. He was how old? Thirty-five? Married?

Whatever had gotten into her? Wondering about such irrelevancies!

When she turned to face him again, he'd stuck his thumbs into the pockets of his jeans. She studied the impressive belt buckle situated exactly between his sinewy hands. It was a large, engraved, silver one. Then she glanced up at his long upper lip framed in deep parenthetical lines. Nice. She had a bias against people with very short upper lips; they looked too much like birds. It was irritating, however, that he was so remote.

"Niall has a pilot's license," said Ruth. "He'll fly us home to Green Lodge."

"You assume that I've already decided to move in with you," Sara said, looking from one to the other.

"Of course you have, my dear," said Ruth. "Foolish of you not to."

"About time to leave," Niall said, and to Sara's surprise, he put a hand under her elbow. Touching her very lightly, he aimed her in the direction of the doorway.

She was ready to raise an eyebrow at him, when the hand suddenly was gone. She cast a last sweeping glance around the hall, wondering where Elmer Snagg was hiding his physical magnificence that surely would be obvious, regardless of what clothes he covered himself with.

Then she studied Niall Whitethorne again and decided

34

he was attractive, too, even if he wasn't much for chitchat. Since he roomed up at Ruth's place, maybe he didn't have an opportunity to talk much. Not easy to get a word in edgewise around Ruth.

Sara and Niall preceded Ruth out of the hall, Sara looking back over her shoulder to see Ruth struggling to finish three concurrent conversations and tear herself away from friends. Dusk was falling in earnest. It's not wise to fly through mountains after dark, Sara knew.

She, too, had a pilot's license. For some reason she didn't want to reveal that fact to Niall Whitethorne.

She was accompanying him down the steps of the hall, looking all about her at the small neat homes within the split-rail fence around the reserve. She didn't ask if he'd ever lived here, for somehow she guessed that he had not. He had been in the town when she first saw him, and now he lived at Green Lodge, where she would stay. . . .

"My luggage has been stashed in the tradestore, locked up overnight," she said, "so I'll need to come to town first thing in the morning for it."

"That can be arranged."

"How far is Green Lodge from here?"

He grinned, an endearing grin that modified the eagle fierceness of his features and gave him almost a boyish look.

"How far on flat land?" he said. "Or how far up? Which do you mean?"

"Oh, yeah. Ruth said her home is on the mountain, didn't she?"

"It sure is. You get to pick between two forms of transport—planes or horses."

"Oops!" Sara opened her mouth to say that under those conditions she couldn't possibly stay at Green Lodge, but Niall spoke first.

"If it were still a hunting lodge, you'd pay a hundred

bucks a night for a room, Sara. Don't be scared off by its location. It's up high, yes, but I can fly you wherever you want to go. That is, if you're still determined to wrestle grizzly bears."

"Not grizzlies, salmon," she said rather testily. Tight-lipped. She didn't look at him, but could feel him staring —probably glaring—down at her. She walked faster.

The view across the valley was lovely, though the sun was out of sight behind the six-thousand-foot mountains that surrounded them. She could see the red roofs of the town beyond the airstrip where the mail plane had landed. No airplane was now visible. The vivid pink fireweed along the river was almost lost in shadow, and the glacier-fed river exhibited only surges of glinting white foam.

Up-valley, Nuhauk Glacier was still brightly sunlit.

And that blasted suspension bridge awaited her.

She must not make a fool of herself, this time, crossing the river. She'd had a bit of practice, and she was, after all, accustomed to unstable high perches that bucked. Today she'd talked the mail pilot into letting her take over the controls of his plane for twenty minutes. She flew the single-engine Bonanza around the jagged peaks of the Coast Range, thrilling at the chop—the turbulence of the heights.

Sara managed to climb the steep wooden steps to the bridge without any visible hesitation, though Niall kept very close behind her. She stepped out almost merrily upon the bridge. Under her boots the meager flooring dropped sickeningly, like a swiftly descending elevator. When Niall and Ruth added their weight as well, Sara closed her eyes for a moment and clenched her teeth. Because she was still carrying her overnight case, it was difficult to get a grip on both flimsy railings. Suddenly a strong, warm hand covered hers and pulled the suitcase away. She did not resist and did not dare to glance over her shoulder at Niall. She wondered where her body would eventually come ashore when the gyrating bridge flipped her off.

"Need any help?" said an infuriating male voice from behind her.

"Nope. Just love it," she lied bravely. "*So* exciting."

She was halfway across. At the lowest point she expected to be drenched in spray, and then she began walking uphill. She accelerated her pace. When she arrived safely on the other side of the river, she felt like a circus aerialist dropping from a trapeze to the welcome security of a platform. What would Niall have done if she'd again dropped to a crouch in the middle of the bridge?

Would strong, handsome hero leap to rescue dainty maiden?

Balderdash! as Dad would say.

She managed nonchalantly to reach for her suitcase, saying, "Thanks a lot. I can carry it now."

"No problem."

"Please, Niall." She said his name for the first time and saw his startled reaction to the sound coming from her lips. She didn't mind hearing him say "Sara" either.

"You are a liberated woman," Niall sighed, but he did not give up the little piece of luggage. She didn't argue.

Ruth dropped back, unable to resist pausing to speak with the next group that had come across the bridge. Niall kept on walking, and so did Sara.

She checked her watch. Ten o'clock here, but at home this was tomorrow. She set the hands back by three hours. Funny that she felt so much less tired now than she had upon her arrival in the valley. A second wind, athletes call it.

"Seen the village totems?" asked Niall.

"Nope, and I'd like to. I also haven't seen a plane on the airfield. What do you fly anyway, a dirigible? The

37

Goodyear blimp? Or do we all crowd onto a broom behind you?"

He cocked an eyebrow at her, clearly puzzled; she felt proud of herself. In her exhausted condition she could summon enough wit to throw this poised, confident man momentarily off balance.

Niall didn't talk to her all the rest of the way to the town, but he led her to the foot of two gigantic totem poles. He watched her staring up at them in awe.

"Those are marvelous."

It was a good thing the light was now a little too dim for her to take good 35-mm slides. She could resist the impulse to jerk out her new camera and play tourist. Behind the totems lay the quiet semi-circle of harbor full of fishing boats.

The totem poles were painted in vivid colors. A sitting bear formed the base of one pole; above him rose a stack of wooden birds with wings like inverted fence pickets. The base of the second totem pole was a long white human face, its mouth open in a red *O*. Niall, seeing her puzzlement, said, "That's Echo."

Above Echo, a black and white killer whale stood upon its head, its tail curved down over its nose like a cup handle.

"And at the top of the totem sits the thunderbird," explained Niall. "Look overhead, and you will see living thunderbirds."

She followed the direction of his pointing finger to see huge hawks making long sweeps over the harbor. Hawks? A dozen hawks? Then she realized they had sleek white heads. He must have heard her gasp, for he grinned.

"Not bald eagles, Niall."

"Why not?"

"I've never seen one outside of a zoo! They're America's national bird."

"Well, these eagles are ours. We haven't poisoned them with chemicals."

Ruth had caught up with them. Panting, she said, "Better climb in the plane, kids, before one of those eagles decides to leave a calling card."

Laughing, Sara looked about her and at last spotted the plane—a blue Beech 18 on floats, a nice little bush plane, marked CG-ALR. She hurried down the dock with Niall to the mooring place of the twin-engine seaplane. He put his hand out to assist her, and only because she was tired Sara took Niall's hand to clamber aboard. It was a tremendously strong hand, but lacked the hard ridge of calluses that she expected. Was he a worker or not? Ruth Bell had certainly said he was her roofer.

She again decided not to mention that she was a pilot. She was far too tired tonight to spend time studying the baffling array of levers in this plane as they taxied out into the harbor, leaving behind the small fishing boats bobbing at anchor.

The town of Chilto was empty, its citizens feasting across the river at Nuhauk Hall. Two tall stacks of totemic creatures stared at them as bald eagles circled in the violet sky.

Normally unsentimental, Sara said to herself gravely, *I've come home. I truly—in a sense—have come home.*

CHAPTER FOUR

Niall buzzed the seaplane along the surface of the little bay and downstream until they'd gained enough speed to leave the water and rise into the air. At the head of the valley, snow packs were shining gold and white in the sun, while the valley below lay in blue shadow. She gazed out the window, catching her breath at the view. One only dreamed of places like this; one didn't get the chance to live in them. Not until now, one didn't!

She'd had no float time at all, and never soloed in a multiengine craft like this one.

On a shoulder of a mountain lay a shimmering blue lake among the vast forests that rose on either side. As Niall circled and came in for a landing, she felt grateful he was the sort of pilot who paid full attention to flying; he did not turn his head to chat with them. Of course Niall Whitethorne was not the sort of man ever to do a lot of chattering. That was part of his charm.

Charm? she asked herself. *Already I've decided this man is charming? Whatever is going on, here, Sara?*

Though she was suppressing a smile, she didn't want to

make any reply to her own question. Didn't dare to, in fact.

Niall did not slide the plane onto the steely surface of the lake as smoothly as a raw egg sliding onto a griddle, as she'd expected. He landed with a tooth-jarring jolt, and Sara wondered whether the lake itself or the pilot was to blame.

She scrambled out of the plane and hopped down onto the dock—without assistance, this time. Her attention was totally captured by the house looming over the lake. That must be Green Lodge.

Its roof, steeply pitched, was covered with rough-cut shingles of dark wood where it wasn't covered with green moss. The roof line was broken by four sets of dormer windows jutting out like gun ports on some antique pirate ship. Around the entrance porch hung curtains of ivy one would have to brush aside to enter. The lodge seemed to lean away from her, the overhang of its deep veranda supported by pillars, each of which was a whole log she could not reach both arms around.

"What a fort!" Sara exclaimed, thinking of the Black Forest. Tall stone chimneys rose like a pair of bookends, pressing the house between them. She pictured blazing hearths, skiing, after-ski lounging . . . and loving.

Behave, Sara. You are here to work. But even while she scolded herself, she smiled.

Niall saw that smile. "You like the place," he said, not asking a question, but making a pronouncement she could not deny.

Even in the blue light of evening she could make out the rainbow-colored patch of flowers growing against the lodge wall.

Niall trotted up the seven wooden steps to the veranda to open the heavy plank door. Her suitcase still swung from his fist.

When she caught up with him and stood in the door-way, she had to stop cold—to stare.

What she expected to find up here was certainly not a musty Victorian parlor.

The attic smell of the interior was a startling contrast to the spicy cedar fragrance of the surrounding forests. Under a ceiling of rough-hewn logs mortared with pale plaster stood chairs upholstered in velvet and plush. Ancient overstuffed furniture crouched among ornate tables with curved legs. A tall breakfront displayed fragile china cups and saucers, none of which matched. Upon the Turkish rug stood a sagging horsehair divan and a love seat with a heart-shaped back.

This might seem an appropriate setting for many old ladies nearing eighty-five, the sort who sit and crochet, but it didn't fit Ruth Bell, that pixie with a sharp tongue who dressed in denim and swaggered like a cowpuncher.

The far end of the parlor was dominated by a silver pot-bellied stove that resembled the armor of a medieval knight. On the walls hung garish paintings on black velvet of elk in the snow and moose languidly wading.

Ruth solved the mystery.

"All the junk crammed in here," she said, "came down through Mr. Bell's family. Awful stuff, but it keeps the room warm. Good insulation."

Sara watched Niall's face but couldn't read his thoughts in it. What Ruth said was obviously making a strong impression on the man, but what sort of impression? The wide mouth remained immobile, but the eyes flashed fire.

Ruth offered them coffee.

"I'd prefer just to head straight to bed and to sleep," said Sara.

Niall was already climbing the stairs, still carrying her overnight case, so she and Ruth followed him up to the

42

second floor. A dormer room opening off the low-ceilinged hall turned out to be hers. Ruth led the way inside.

When the light flared in a hurricane lamp on the bedside table, it illuminated walls of polished golden logs contrasting with immaculate white mortar. Ruth opened the bed, revealing white sheets beneath a crazy quilt of brocade and velvet squares. *Great-grandmothers make quilts like that, and museums preserve them,* Sara mused groggily. The bed was a four-poster, of course, and proclaimed its advanced age by the height of its mattress from the floor.

"Myself, I need a footstool to climb up into these old beds," Ruth said. The way the old woman's bleary blue eyes moved from Sara to Niall, Sara expected her to ask Niall to hoist her small guest into the bed. Blessedly, Ruth only said, "I'll go fill the bathtub; you want a bath, surely, child."

"Child" certainly did want a bath. As she opened the overnight case that Niall set on the dresser, she wondered when the man would depart. He showed no inclination to go.

"Excuse me," Sara said, which elicited a smile from him, plus a raised eyebrow. He didn't move, however. She told herself to go ahead and unpack and ignore him.

It was easy enough to unpack her toiletries, robe, and slippers, but when she began to pull out the flannelette gown, she stopped. Her friends had given her the gown as a joke, back in steamy-hot Lexington, Kentucky, on the tenth day of August, three days—no, eons—ago.

It was a floor-length royal blue gown warm enough for cool British Columbia nights, but she tried to keep Niall from seeing what had happened to its formerly modest neckline. Her friend Jay-Dean had done surgery on it, removing the buttoned panel to leave a plunging neckline. Then she had edged the décolleté with rows of gathered lace. At one of the bon voyage parties another friend had held up this creation and sent the gang into giggles by saying, "If Sara must go to bed in Canada looking like Grandma Moses from behind, she sure can look like Marie Antoinette in front!"

Sara folded the nightgown up quickly inside her rose-colored velour robe and draped them both over her arm. Ruth reappeared, laden with towels, which she hung over Sara's other arm.

"Follow me to the bathroom," she said, completely ignoring Niall. "Then, I rather think that a mug of hot chocolate might hit the spot, am I right, lass?"

"You're a perfect angel, Ruth."

"Angel? Hmpf!" she retorted.

Niall, with those arching brows and chisled face, looked like a tantalizing demon, Sara thought as she followed Ruth down the hall to a door decorated with a panel of stained glass. Inside, she found herself, for the first time in two decades, entering a Canadian bathroom. She now remembered that old Canadian homes have separate rooms for toilet and for bath. This lovely room was meant only for bathing and dressing. It was lit not by any glaring overhead light fixture, but by a softly glowing table lamp on a dressing table.

The dressing table also held a gilt-edged oval mirror that reflected a bouquet of huge pink and yellow begonias. A white sheepskin rug half covered the floor. The white porcelain washbasin was the size of a birdbath, and the tub, up on lion-paw feet, was immensely long and deep. It was filling up with bubbles and steam. The fragrance of jasmine was stupefying. Sara brushed damp hair off her forehead.

"Oh, my," she said, "I could swim laps in that tub."

"You don't imagine you might fall asleep while bathing and drown?" asked Ruth with real concern.

"Not a chance."

Sara spoke too soon. The combination of heat, jasmine fumes, and her long travels was becoming too much. The moment after Ruth rushed away to make the hot chocolate, Sara's legs collapsed under her. She managed to sit down just in time on the cushioned stool in front of the dressing table.

Had Ruth Bell retained her youth and vigor by dashing up and down those steep stairs all day long? Sara wondered.

Suddenly, in the still-open bathroom door, Niall appeared. He looked at the brimming tubful of bubbles, glanced at Sara, and shook his head as if confronted with a total incompetent. Before Sara could say anything he came into the room, strode across the sheepskin, and turned off both faucets on the tub.

"Thank you," she said. "You've been very considerate, and tomorrow I'll be in better shape—"

"Nothing wrong with your sh—" he began, and stopped himself before she had to. But he didn't depart. He approached Sara, took the towels from off her arm, and hung both of them across the bar above the tub. He next dropped the washcloth into the bubbles and placed a soapdish from the basin on the appropriate rack over the tub. Then he stood facing Sara with a bemused expression on his face.

"Thanks again," she said, thinking how little he looked like either a gentleman's valet or a lady's maid. His efficiency was intimidating. There she sat like a zombie, gazing at that tempting tubful of hot water, and there stood Niall, unable to do anything further to aid her toward her goal. Well, not unable, but awaiting permission to be even more helpful.

She did manage to twist around and place her robe and nightgown upon the dresser behind her. Then her empty arms fell limp by her sides, her right hand releasing her bedroom slippers, which hit the rug with a *clunk*.

The jasmine scent was overpowering. Ruth had put in far too much bubble bath. Is there such a thing as a love potion absorbed through the nasal membranes? Sara began to wonder.

"You might go now, Niall. I have to get undressed."

"Is MacFarland Scottish or Irish?" he unexpectedly demanded. "Your name," he clarified.

"MacFarland? Scottish. My dad is pure Scottish."

"Mine was Irish," he said.

Now, that explained the exotic name Niall, but—

"Irish? Whitethorne?" she inquired.

He didn't answer. In fact, he seemed sorry that he'd blurted out anything about his ancestry. Sara could not help visualizing a dashing Irish adventurer—named, say, Patrick O'Reilly—exploring these forests and wooing a lovely Indian maiden. Was the maiden's family named Whitethorne?

Sara tried to keep her eyes focussed on his face while her fingers blindly sought the buttons of her vest. She undid them, one by one.

Niall, without a word, suddenly moved nearer, put his fingers lightly on her shoulders and lifted the vest down and off her arms. *It looks as if he's had plenty of practice undressing women,* Sara thought. He came around in front of her again, carrying the vest folded over his arm. He then knelt on one knee, like an old-fashioned gentleman about to propose. His behavior fit the age and decor of the house, but did not fit his lumberjack costume of flannel and denim or the knowing expression in his eyes.

Grasping the left heel of her brown leather boot, he tugged on it. She clung to the edge of the stool, leaned back, and slowly dragged her foot out of the boot. She might indeed have had trouble getting her boots off without aid. Score one for Niall Whitethorne. He motioned for her other foot, and she gave it to him so he could tug off that boot as well.

Still no comment from him, though his eyes never ceased talking to her. He remained on one knee, gazing at her travel-rumpled yellow shirt, her denim jeans, and her slumped shoulders. He turned his sleek head toward the bathtub, and then looked at Sara again with quizzical amusement.

"You doubt that I can manage to move from here to that tub, don't you?" she said.

"Exactly. I have never before seen anyone quite as paralyzed by weariness as you are."

"I'm asphixiated by the perfume," she said lightly, hiding her irritation at her odd response to Niall's nearness. His body gave off a spicy fragrance far more pleasant than the jasmine. One would think that he himself had very recently bathed. Her inhibitions slipping, she fought the temptation to touch his smooth golden jawline, to run a fingertip down the straight, slim nose. It was a good thing she was too tired to lift a hand, but a bad thing that she wasn't too tired to imagine this man opening his arms and embracing her, pulling her down with him onto the soft, white sheepskin. To sleep. *Not* to make love!

The next moment she proved herself a liar. Desire began to fill Sara's body. She wondered if he had any notion of her feelings. He looked like a man assured of himself, of his sexual appeal, and of his prowess.

She shivered.

"I can manage," she murmured.

"Manage to crawl to the tub maybe, but not to get yourself undressed. I'd say you need still more help, Sara."

"Sorry, buster!" she heard herself say, using slang of her mother's generation. "Buzz off!"

He laughed at her. Still on one knee on the sheepskin

rug, he laughed merrily, but did not move. He also did not try to overpower her and strip her naked. That scenario was in both their minds, but Niall, remaining motionless, said, "I can revive you very quickly, Sara, with your permission. I can wake you up."

"How?" she asked suspiciously.

"Do I have your permission to try, or shall I just undress you and drop you into the tub? I certainly wouldn't mind doing that. It's up to you."

He still crouched very close to her knees.

No doubt, any agile, strong man of his size could strip her and dunk her in the hot water before she could protest. Her traitorously limp body wouldn't have to move one muscle. It was a tempting thought, but certainly no way to begin a relationship that must remain platonic. She was a rational scientist, no slave to emotion, and she would not succumb to her unwelcome, inappropriate erotic reactions to a stranger.

Waiting for her answer, Niall grew impatient. He put three fingers on her top shirt button, brushing his hand against her breasts, and twisted the button out of its hole.

"Just better back off, friend," she said, grabbing his wrist and finding herself unable to twist it at all.

"Then there's only the less pleasant alternative, Sara. Less pleasant for you as well as for me."

She noticed how fluent and articulate he had become—this silent man. She watched him rise from his knee and push up one shirt-sleeve to expose a shapely, tanned forearm wound with prominent veins. He went over to the bathtub, fished the washcloth out of the water, and carried the dripping wet ball of cloth to the washbasin. He turned on the tap, and he waited.

She waited too, perplexed.

Then Niall came back over to Sara, roping the wet cloth

between his hands. Without a word of warning, he did his cruel duty.

He slapped the icy cold washcloth violently across her neck. Across the base of her naked throat.

"You—"

The shock jerked her upright on the stool. Flinging both hands against his chest, kicking both legs by reflex, she missed a damaging blow to his body. Her feet now underneath her, she sprang up.

Niall leaped out of her path.

"That'll work every time," he drawled, as if he made his living not repairing roofs but reviving women. He tossed the cold washcloth over his shoulder, so it flew in an arc into the tub.

"GO!" Sara shouted, pointing to the door. "Enough is more than enough!"

She tried to act angry. In fact, she was trying not to giggle. Though the cold-rag treatment hurt, it certainly succeeded. She was alert now. What a man! He did exactly what he said he would. She felt as wide awake as she'd been while watching the rain dance in Nuhauk Hall.

Niall made a curt little bow, turned, and went out of the door, closing it behind him.

Sara hurried to latch the bathroom door, wriggled out of her shirt, pants, and underwear, and crawled over the high wall of the tub.

She sank with a groan of pleasure into the hot water, until she was immersed to her chin. The washcloth swam like a fish around her knees as she rubbed hot, wet hands over her face. What an experience! She should have grabbed the cold washcloth he'd slapped her with and stuck it right in his eye! She enjoyed another fit of giggles, blowing bubbles away from her lips down the length of the tub. The tub was so long that she could have lain in it at full length underwater. Like a rowboat. Two could bathe in it at once.

She'd scrubbed herself thoroughly before she heard rapping at the door. She reared up to see Ruth's small silhouette through the stained-glass ferns and tulips.

"I brought your nightcap, Sara," said Ruth's voice through the door. "Don't move. None of these old latches hold."

Ruth gave the door a kick to burst it open.

Sara sank.

Ruth offered her a red ceramic mug, which Sara grasped in both hands.

"You are a darling, Ruth, and a marvel. I don't know about your friend Niall, but at least life at Green Lodge promises to be eventful."

For once the old woman remained silent. When Ruth departed, Sara lay back and sipped the bittersweet chocolate in which a melting marshmallow was sailing. Mom used to do that—drop marshmallows into cups of hot chocolate for her and her brothers. She felt like a kid again, one with a doting grandma and a devilish older brother. But there was nothing brotherly in the way Niall Whitethorne looked at her, in the way he moved so sinuously, gracefully. Lionlike.

One good night's sleep, and she'd get to work. She had to stop being so foolish.

Niall would be kept busy hammering shingles on this roof, high on the mountain, while Sara, down in the valley, would deal with the salmon and the grizzlies. She'd practiced handling heavy, slippery fish at a Kentucky fish hatchery. Now all she needed was to hire some help and unpack her aluminum trunks stowed in the tradestore in town. The syringes and other glassware had been spared a fifth plane ride; they would go into a room in town that she'd rent and convert into a tiny laboratory.

For the second stage of her work, Green Lodge had rooms galore. She'd equip a lab up here when she dealt with salmon in the higher-elevation streams.

Sara contemplated the myriad rainbow-tinted bubbles, the empty red mug, and the tall white sides of the tub. All she had to do now was climb out of this giant bathtub, find her bedroom again, and climb up into bed. Ruefully, she admitted she was a small person. Strong, but not nearly as strong as most men. She had to use her wits. Starting tomorrow. Tonight, needing Niall's help, she'd acted more like a half-wit. But no harm done. His opinion didn't matter to her in the least.

Men versus women! Conventional wisdom says men make their major commitment in life to their work. Women are supposed to make a deep commitment only to a man. Not necessarily so, Niall Whitethorne notwithstanding.

CHAPTER FIVE

Sara awoke to a silent house and to sunshine, saying a mental thank-you to Niall for postponing his hammering. Her dormer room lay directly under the steeply sloping roof.

Twenty to eight, said her watch, so perhaps the man wouldn't have been starting his work this early in the morning anyway. Lying diagonally across the bed, Sara stretched both arms above her head and pointed her toes like a diver. Time to dive in. It was August 14, and the salmon were beginning their spawning run. She certainly felt no more jet lag, so—*no more malingering, Sara!*

A rattle of footsteps sounded on the stairs, and soon after she heard a tapping at her door. Niall? So early? Before she could decide whether seeing him would be a good or bad start for her day, the door opened, and Ruth peeked in, grinning. Sara hauled herself up in bed.

The courtesan's nightgown, slit nearly to her navel, didn't come along with her. It fell off her shoulders.

Ruth had turned her head to speak with someone behind her while Sara struggled with her nightgown. Hoisting herself off the mattress, she dragged it into place again, more or less. Though she was small, she had a considerable amount of bosom to cover.

She clawed her fingers uselessly through her hair. Hopeless.

Who cares, she thought.

"Good morning?" she said to Ruth Bell's back.

A wrinkled mask of hilarity faced her again, making Sara add, "What's wrong? I mean, what's so funny this morning?"

"Just now wake up?" asked Ruth.

"Sure did. A wonderful night's sleep."

"Breakfast is served," Ruth responded. "You must be starved."

"Breakfast in bed?"

Sara was immensely pleased. In the MacFarland household only the miserably ill got meals served to them, and she was never ill. It was only polite to respond, "Why, you shouldn't have!" so she said it, chuckling to herself because she didn't mean a word of it. She only hoped that her hostess-landlady didn't give herself a heart attack lugging food upstairs for an athletic, young, nonpaying guest.

"Don't thank me. I didn't cook it. Bettina did."

Sara didn't ask who Bettina was or where Niall was. Holding the neckline of her gown closed, she was on her way to snatch her robe from a nearby chair when someone else joined Ruth in the bedroom.

In stalked Niall, half hidden by a bed tray the size of a small table. Sara scrambled back into bed without her robe to cover her.

With a wicked grin he raked his gaze over her disarranged décolleté. He had to bend over Sara to place the tray across her middle, and the lascivious gaze aimed at Jay-Dean's lacework both amused and inflamed Sara.

She found she could ignore Niall, however, when she discovered what the bed tray contained.

A blue crockery platter held three fried eggs, and beside them reclined a steak big enough for suppertime. There was a bowl of multi-colored berries, a fragrant mug of steaming coffee, and even buttered toast and marmalade.

Sara shook out the linen napkin and quickly bunched it like a cravat into her neckline. Then she decided to try to eat her huge Canadian breakfast Canadian-style, holding her fork in her left hand while she kept the knife in her right. Ruth and Niall watched her with interest.

Her uneducated left hand, unfortunately, did not cooperate, and most of her food fell off her fork.

Ruth and Niall, enjoying this exhibition, both howled.

"Go on, be a Yank," Ruth said. "Throw your fork from hand to hand, Sara. It's kinda cute."

Niall added, "You'll need a lot of blubber on you, so finish it all."

She knew that was a reference to her work in the cold river and its feeder streams, but she continued to ignore him. The food was delicious; she couldn't eat it fast enough. How famished she was! Breakfast was not only wonderful, but the tray satisfied her artistic taste as well—nicely color-coordinated. The red huckleberries, raspberries, and blackberries mixed with blueberries looked too pretty to eat, but their stinging sweetness helped wake her up.

"You won't need to hang around, Ruth," Niall said boldly, as if Ruth were his employee rather than the reverse. "I'll wait for her to finish."

"Whatever for?" asked Sara, sitting up in the high bed like a small, hungry queen. She watched the man push the door shut behind Ruth's obediently retreating figure. Today Niall wore a neatly pressed khaki shirt and trousers that made him look like a soldier or a forest ranger. He removed her robe from the chair, spun the chair around and sat down, straddling the seat, his arms crossed, resting on the chairback.

"Now tell me what insanity you expect to attempt up here in B.C.," Niall commanded.

"I am eating," she tried to say in spite of a full mouth, irritated at such arrogance. What was he anyway? Who was he? He wasn't being polite any longer. Curiosity was natural, but he was acting almost boorish.

She told him so. "I don't see what business it is of yours, frankly."

"I got here first," he said.

"Well, great! You attend to your roof, and I'll attend to my salmon. Agreed?"

"Who'll fly you down the mountain?"

"I'll go down on a horse if I must. You mentioned that was a viable alternative."

Again she chose to keep secret the fact that she had a pilot's license, but that skill wouldn't help her much today. Unfortunately, she was not licensed to fly a seaplane, and from the air she'd seen no airstrip on the mountain for a conventional aircraft.

"You ought to see the breakneck horse trail," he said. "How's your vertigo? I seem to remember you didn't much like the suspension bridge over the river."

"Well, I—"

She said no more, struck with the foolishness of her decision to lodge up here. Why had she accepted Ruth's offer of a free room with a view? Transportation problems would do her in. This man was going to bargain with her, possibly refuse flatly to give her a ride to town in the plane. Could Ruth force him to do so? Sara hated to have to run to Ruth like a little tot running to Grandma to be rescued from a tormenting brother.

She regarded him coldly. "Of course, I don't expect

favors from you, Niall." She almost called him Mr. White-thorne, but curbed her impulse to be snide. "I am perfectly willing to pay you for your time when I fly in Ruth's seaplane." She emphasized the word *Ruth's*.

He did not say anything, but continued drilling that hot, dark gaze through her until she wondered if the pillows piled up behind her would ignite. *Just make sure, Sara, that you yourself don't ignite,* she heard her mind caution her body.

"Niall, I don't wish to take up any more of your valu-able time, when you already have another job. Why don't you leave, and I can take this tray back downstairs. Then you can go about your duties."

"I haven't heard an answer to my question," he said blithely, as if he owned Green Lodge. "What mischief are you planning in regard to the valley's hapless salmon?"

Hapless salmon? She marveled at his vocabulary. She didn't often meet that quaint adjective outside of books. Or had he said *hopeless* salmon, and she'd misunderstood him? Her puzzlement seemed to amuse him.

"Come on, Sara. Eat your food. I'll take the tray back down for you. You won't be able to get out from under it."

"I sure can."

She dug into the rest of the breakfast, slugged down the coffee so fast it burned her throat, and got a grip on each side of the homemade wooden tray. She hoisted it.

It was so heavy, she could barely lift it off the quilt, and then her legs were in the way. Sara's difficulties with the tray made Niall's eyes dance with delight. Then the shoul-ders of her gown started sliding again. The tray sagged, the dishes clattered, and she grabbed for her neckline with both hands.

Niall was on his feet, reaching for the tray, his face not far above hers, studying with interest her half-exposed breasts. She hated the way she colored as he took the tray off her thighs, moving very slowly, staring at her all the while. He moistened his lips, and his brows arched over those penetrating eyes.

After he put the tray on the chiffoniere he neatly pivoted in place and leaned over Sara again. The stack of pillows sagged as he planted a hand on each side of her head.

"Sara, why not admit you'd like a little dessert after that big meal?"

His voice was so soft that she barely heard him.

"You don't get dessert with breakfast," she heard herself reply as two big hands closed upon her shoulders, caressing, moving the blue lace-edged fabric back and forth against her flesh. Dessert. Niall was about to kiss her.

He rested his hip on the edge of the bed, moving in, smelling of shaving lotion, toothpaste, cologne—good smells. He gripped her shoulders more and more tightly, sliding the gown down so a bit more of her breasts showed. Then he took possession of her parted lips in the middle of her gasp.

Sara waited too long to lift her hands in resistance. Now her arms were pinned by her sides. She was silenced by his demanding mouth as he put more of his weight upon her half-reclining body. He groaned with pleasure, moving his mouth down the side of her neck, along her collarbone, and burying his warm face between her half-exposed breasts.

"Oh, Niall!" she gasped, wanting this, hating the realization that she did not want to struggle.

Even if she fought him and he overpowered her, silenced her cries with his mouth, jerked the bedclothes aside, and joined her in this bed, she felt sure of one thing. She'd be forced into an ecstasy that up to now had been denied her. Denied her by her mother's warnings, her own doubts and inhibitions, and by the fumbling lovemaking of men she'd known. This man would not make love by the book. She was sure of that, but she was equally sure that now was not the time for her to find out.

"Please, don't," she managed to whisper.

"You mean that?" he said, pulling a little away.

"Why, you've been hurt!" she suddenly exclaimed, pushing open Niall's collar. Peculiar lacerations crossed both of his collarbones.

Then she realized that he'd surely take this as an invitation to undress. But instead of shrugging out of his shirt, Niall drew back, clutching his collar closed. He acted exactly like her as she clutched her own neckline together. She couldn't help bursting into laughter at the bold man's inexplicable modesty.

"Why, Niall! Whatever is wrong?"

The momentary pause in his lovemaking—"his" because she'd been too startled to respond—gave her strength to sit up farther in bed and quiz him.

"What are you hiding, Niall?"

"What are *you* hiding?" he said confusingly.

He slid off the bed, turned away from her, and picked up the bed tray.

"Another time, Sara," he said firmly.

She could not help noticing, just below the bed tray, proof that his eagerness had not abated.

"By the way," he said in a more cheerful tone of voice, "notice the time, Sara?"

She checked the watch she wore even to bed. "Eight-ten."

"You don't know east from west, do you, Yankee?"

"What do you mean?"

"Notice how the light is failing?"

"Failing? It's gonna rain today? Darn it!"

"You sure get confused, woman scientist. It's coming on to sunset."

"What?" She rose straight up in bed, drawing her legs under her. "What are you saying?"

"Sunset."

"Sunset? Breakfast? You fed me eggs . . ." she spluttered. "I've slept all *day*? All night and all *day*?"

"Sure looks like it."

He resisted laughing out loud, but on sides of his tightly closed mouth a pair of creases deepened.

"I sure must've needed the sleep," she muttered, suppressing laughter in her amazement.

"Yeah. As I somehow recall, you could scarcely get into your bathtub last night—twenty-some hours ago."

Holding the bed tray balanced on one palm—an impressive demonstration of weightlifting—Niall headed for the door and pulled it open.

"If I'd helped you a little more last night—say joined you in that bathtub—Sara, you wouldn't be awake, even yet."

She made a face at him behind his back.

"Conceited!" she said.

"Don't judge something until you've tried it," he said, and left the room, kicking the door firmly closed behind him.

CHAPTER SIX

Sara refused to stay in bed. It would be absurd after all that sleep. She had nothing to work with except contour maps showing the locations of the streams, but she could dress and go downstairs and talk to Ruth Bell about her transportation problems. She could also find out what the status of Niall Whitethorne was around here. Ruth would surely know a lot about him.

Sara didn't want to think about that kiss. She was not the kind of woman to encourage strangers to kiss her, especially to kiss her in bed. How long, she wondered, was a man a stranger before he could be called a friend?

It might be interesting to creep downstairs and listen to the two of them, Ruth and Niall, laughing at her, slapping their thighs over the Yank who could lose twelve hours of her life without missing them.

She jumped down from the bed and slid out of the nightgown on which she'd have to sew a few buttons. She got into her sole change of clothes—wine-colored jeans and an Icelandic gray wool sweater. It was very obvious now that night was falling. How had Ruth been able to resist seeing Sara's astonished face when she discovered the time?

Sara didn't find anyone in the dim kitchen, but she relished her exploring trip. The size of the walk-in pantry and the length of the steel kitchen counters proved that this had been a lodge for many guests. She opened a creaking, cast-iron door in the woodstove to see that it was still full of glowing coals. The wide dining room was unheated and chilly under its moose-antler chandeliers sporting light bulbs.

At the far end of a long, dark hall, Sara sensed life stirring. She decided not to eavesdrop at the door, but pushed it open, bathing herself in the warm, golden light from within. There were no lights on in this little parlor, she realized. The source of both heat and illumination was a huge stone fireplace.

Niall lounged before that fire, his back against a hassock and his long legs stretched out upon a bearskin rug. A skinned bear in the sitting room, and a dead sheep in the bathroom, Sara thought in amusement. That, of course was in addition to the animals stacked on totem poles and the bald eagles down in the valley. She liked it. How much she liked this saturnine male in the house, she wasn't quite sure. At least he wasn't the only one. Ruth was here too.

The great stone fireplace had a raised hearth, on which orange and blue flames licked at logs as hefty as human thighs. The tawny rug on which Niall sat was complete with a threatening head and jaws parted to show sharp white teeth. Four spread-eagled legs ended in curved claws four inches long. Sara glanced from the bear's scowl up to Niall's and decided to greet Ruth instead of him.

Ruth Bell was waiting, suppressing a grin, as she perched on the sofa. A book was open upon her lap.

"I appreciate the humor of your little joke," Sara began,

61

"but if that's the sort of breakfast you serve around here, I dread seeing the feast you lay on at midday."

"We'll fatten you up, rest assured," said Ruth. "Speaking of rest, I'm headed for the sack now myself. Niall can keep you company. Gave him a day off work, today, you did. We couldn't have him pounding nails right on top of Sleeping Beauty. So he owes you something."

"Not at all," Sara remarked, before Niall could mention what kind of reward he might want.

Sara asked, "That's a grizzly, isn't it? The rug? It's such a pale color, almost beige."

"Silver-tipped," said Niall.

Ruth didn't rush to depart.

"I'll have to tell Sara about my own bear," she said. "Not that one. Mine is up in my bedroom. My bear was stealing our garbage and even fruit off the trees, right in the daytime. It was after my old man died. That bear got so bold that I got cross with it. Found myself a twenty-two rifle and hit him right in the eye. There's no other way to kill a grizzly with a twenty-two. Gracious, did I make friends quick, after that! People don't accept you in this valley till your family's been here two generations, but I was accepted overnight after I plugged that grizzly."

"Don't you ever try a trick like that again," warned Niall sternly. "Or you either, Sara. Neither of you is a hunter."

"I don't fool around with guns," Sara reassured him.

"Take more'n a bear to kill a Holmstrom—that was my maiden name, Holmstrom," said Ruth. "You scare Sara good, Niall. She's got a whole life ahead of her, and we can't have her taking chances. Good night, you two," she said, and departed.

When she'd been gone for about two minutes, Niall arose, went to the door, opened it, peered out, and then shut it again. He walked past the fireplace to a liquor cabinet.

"What'll you have?" he asked Sara from the shadows.

"Well, since my breakfast was really supper, and you said I was due a dessert, I'll take a creme-de-something or an amaretto, if there's anything like that. That'll be all the dessert I'll need tonight."

His face indicated that he caught her meaning, and he didn't lay a finger on her as he brought her an aperitif that smelled sweetly of almonds.

"Now," he said, sitting down on the bearskin once more, holding a wineglass in his fingers, "I'm serious about the dangers you face up here, Sara. Starting with bears."

"I suspect that Professor Whitethorne's lecture is about to begin," she said, her expression placid, as if she were not baiting him at all. Then she relented.

"How big was this bear you're sitting on?" she asked, deciding the best way to keep him from making a move toward her in this romantic setting was to keep him talking. Besides, they needed to get better acquainted.

"It weighed nearly a thousand pounds. The head's twenty-six inches across. It's a record for this area. It was shot back when I was a kid."

"You lived here as a kid?"

"Yeah. My dad was the hunting guide out of Green Lodge. He would've killed animals only for food for his family. But the rich hunters he had to guide—" Niall snorted.

"They wanted trophies, huh?"

He nodded.

"I'll bet you have some harrowing stories to tell."

She didn't foresee a response, so she added, "Ruth said there was no TV up here, so you'll have to furnish the entertainment."

For a moment Sara wondered if Niall would purposely misunderstand her meaning, but he took a sip of his wine and then launched into a hunting story. She listened to his low voice with acute interest.

"Once when I was about twelve, we had a Yank shoot a sow grizzly must've weighed forty-five stone. Six hundred fifty pounds in Yank terms," Niall explained. "He just wounded her, poor thing, so we went back the next day to find her. You find bloodstains in the moss by rubbing it between your fingers. We found hollows where she rested, and then the tracks stopped, so we knew she was somewhere near, waiting for us."

"Wow," Sara said involuntarily. "How many of you were there?"

"Dad and I and a Yank bow hunter who wanted a go at it."

"What happened?"

"My father hadn't cocked his rifle, when here comes the bear, rushing through the trees. Dad slipped and fell backwards, nearly shooting me, and the bloody bear stepped right on his leg. I was trying to cock my gun while I was rolling downslope, and the bear jumped right over me. The bow-and-arrow hunter looked like a violinist, drawing, then letting go, drawing, and letting the string go slack, back and forth on the bow. Dad said run, so I ran. Shooting from the hip with a thirty-thirty, Dad got the bear. Put the poor beast out of her pain."

"Quite a dad to have! That was twenty years ago?"

"Just about," he said, realizing she was calculating his age. So what? He knew her age.

So Niall Whitethorne was near thirty-two or thereabouts, Sara thought. She did not want to ask his marital history yet.

She didn't have to. He supplied her with all the information she wanted.

"I'm thirty-one and not married, never have been," he said, staring into her eyes without blinking. "Anything else you want to know?"

She resisted saying, Everything. Niall was sharp. Nothing got past him. He was proving an interesting opponent to spar with.

"Are you trying to scare me off, or is there really a bear problem nowadays?" she asked him. "I was not given statistical data on the bear population when I—"

"How about grizzlies on the road up the valley standing up, twelve feet tall, stopping traffic like policemen so their cubs can cross the road? Yeah, I'm serious about the bears around here, but don't label it a problem. You're the problem. The bears belong here. You do not."

"Gee, thanks."

He didn't respond, so she couldn't just sit there looking into her amaretto or looking at the long lean length of him and that captivating Irish-Indian face. She tried again.

"I'm quite familiar with black bears in the Smokies," she said. "The Great Smoky Mountains National Park in North Carolina."

"Grow up, Sara!" Niall snapped. "Grizzlies are a different species entirely from little black bears. Look, we all go into the woods, but we know what can happen. Can't you do your studies in deeper water where it's less dangerous? Near to town?"

"You certainly don't understand my research."

"You'll understand my warnings when you see the next grizzly victim—some woman who was washing clothes in a river or some kid who just happened to be picking the wrong berries. You wear perfume, I notice. That upsets bears."

"And your shaving lotion doesn't?"

He ignored that. He sat forward, arms linked around his knees. She studied his fringed leather moccasins and his hard brown hands, grasping each other as—not an hour ago—they'd grasped her shoulders. Remembering that, she tried not to shiver.

"Look, Sara, you need instruction. Number one, suppose you come upon a bear. They're half deaf and half blind, and you can bump into them before you or they know it. Would you run?"

"Sure, I'd run. Definitely."

He shook his head in obvious disgust. "Then you're dead. They can roar along at thirty miles an hour."

"Then what do you suggest?"

"Lie down, cross your arms up over your head, and pray."

"I'd prefer to climb a tree."

"You better have a climbable tree nearby and get up it very fast."

"Do you suggest that I carry a gun?"

"No. I suggest that you have a man with a big-game rifle watching over you every minute you're on the streams. Every single day."

Niall shoved another log into the fireplace, causing sparks to cascade over the hearth. Then he sank back against the hassock again, stubbornly silent. Brooding. She had the unpleasant feeling that he was absolutely right.

"Okay. I'll consider your advice."

"Tell me about your project," he commanded.

It was eleven P.M., when Niall went upstairs to bed. His room was just two doors down from Sara's. Why hadn't Ruth put Sara in the bedroom right beside his? Sharing a common wall, he could have listened to Sara getting undressed, and she could listen to him snore, if he did snore.

The saucier Sara acted, the more engrossed he became.

66

After the bear stories he'd told her, she'd told him about her father the accountant, her three brothers, and her legal-secretary mother. And how she was due back in the States on the fifteenth of September.

Niall sat up in bed, chilled by the cold sheets, unable to start reading either of the half-finished technical tomes lying on the bedtable. He kept picturing Sara—Sara half asleep in the bathroom, Sara losing her delicious seductress's gown, Sara bundled in the Icelandic sweater, letting him know he was not to kiss her again, but giving no clue why not. She wasn't by any means a cold woman.

Better lay off her, he supposed. He hadn't come back to the valley to have a one-month fling with a Yank scientist who was going to return to Kentucky for the rest of her life—if she didn't end up as mincemeat before the month was out.

He'd enjoyed hearing her patiently explain her work to him, thinking he couldn't understand much of it. She asked him for pen and paper so she could diagram a hypothetical stream that fed into the Nuhauk River. In the river the salmon were plump, healthy, and sexually mature, she told him gravely, as if he hadn't known that by the age of four.

In the tributary streams the salmon deteriorated. He'd known that all his life too. He'd caught salmon before and after they grew humps on their backs, fungus on their sides, and hooks on their upper jaws like the beaks of parrots. In recent years he had learned about the pituitary gland's overactivity that sends the fish into a biochemical tailspin.

Sara MacFarland, B.S., M.S., didn't have to lecture him on the subject, though he'd encouraged her to do so. Very soon she'd receive her Ph.D. degree, but he was sure he knew almost as much about the salmon as she did.

She even used the analogy that he expected—a comparison between the fast-aging salmon and kids recently in the news who suffered from progeria. Kids of eight with eighty-year-old bodies, sad little mysteries of nature.

Ruth should have stayed downstairs and listened. Wait till she heard that "dear little Sara" was into gerontology. Ruth confidently looked forward to celebrating her hundredth birthday.

Niall cursed himself for acting as if he didn't know what Sara was talking about. He'd faked a perpetually puzzled expression. He'd asked her what amino acids were and how you assay for them. He got a physiology lecture when he would have much preferred to be lying beside her in bed.

Her institute down in Kentucky ought to have known better. They should have sent a couple of brawny men to do this project, not one small woman. She'd need a lot more muscle than she had. The little thing couldn't even get her boots off by herself last night, or get out from under the bed tray tonight. Just hand her a forty-pound fighting salmon!

Niall groaned, switched off the bedside light, and slid, shivering, down between the icy sheets. When she'd decided to head upstairs to bed, he'd made a move, and she'd deflected it, staring bravely up into his eyes, saying, "No, Niall. I don't know you well enough. In fact I hardly know you at all."

How right she was. All that he'd told her about himself was true, but he sure hadn't told her everything. He regretted all the deceit, starting with the rain dance, but it was too late to do anything about it. She wasn't the sort of woman to forgive a man for putting on a masquerade that would make her feel like a fool.

One thing he did know for sure. He knew exactly who

was going to guard Sara when she did her salmon study. Whether she liked it or not. Whatever it might lead to between the two of them.

"After all, Sara," he said softly, "we can't have you getting yourself killed. You are far too intelligent and tantalizing."

CHAPTER SEVEN

Sara smiled wistfully as she thought of her long conversation with Niall the night before. She lay in bed looking at the sunrise, and recalled how quickly Niall caught on when she explained technical terms like serum analysis and thyroxin. He listened intently, never taking his eyes off her. Hardly saying a thing about his own background or interests, he soaked up two hours of her explanation of physiology.

In the morning she got dressed and was outside the lodge by six A.M. No sign of Niall. The sun was up, warming the air and melting the morning fog down the forested slopes of the mountains. The river and town three thousand feet below her were still submerged in a dense white mist like some frozen sea.

She had on blue shorts, jogging shoes, and a bright orange T-shirt as she took off around the lake, planning to circle it once before she went in and raided the Green Lodge refrigerator. This temperature, altitude, and latitude kept her famished; a half-mile run wouldn't be nearly enough to kill her appetite, as running usually did.

She paused halfway around the lake to peer over sheer cliffs into the mist-filled valley. Then she continued her jog along the terrace basin of the mountain. Blue water reflected sky, and fish blew bubbles to the surface. She suspected it was ice-water, like the water of the glacier-fed river.

But when Sara put her fingertips into the glistening ripples, she smiled in surprise. Not frigid at all! Warm! Its temperature must be as high as sixty-five or seventy degrees. Warm enough for swimming.

She hadn't thought of bringing a bathing suit to Canada, for she knew the salmon river would be cold, and one does not swim in shallow tributaries among the amorous salmon. She had not expected to be living beside a lake.

But work before play, she reminded herself. This morning she'd somehow have to get down to the town again to hire a helper or two. No use dreaming that by herself she could lift thirty-pound salmon still in peak condition, fiercely fighting and slippery as well. Later on, upstream, when the fish prematurely aged, she would be able to do the catching by herself.

With or without an armed guard? She hoped she wouldn't have to spend extra funds on a rifleman. The thought did enter her head of hiring Niall Whitethorne, but he had a job already. He'd surely prefer working up here in the dry sunshine to doing back-breaking labor down in the river. Shingles were already stacked between the dormer widows, waiting to be hammered into place. Besides, Ruth needed Niall, and Niall might be an obstreperous employee for a young woman to handle. He seemed too eager to handle her anyway.

She knew from experience how hard it is to date a man whom you work beside every day. At the lab, personal power struggles could become horrendous, involving everything from who makes the coffee to who gets senior authorship on joint papers.

She continued her invigorating jog, drawing in deep, rhythmic breaths. This was the sweetest-smelling air she'd ever breathed. Smog-free, it blew straight over the Pacific and up the long fjord without a hint of exhaust fumes or even of dead fish. Pristine.

As she completed her brisk circuit of the lake, jogging on a path springy with fir and spruce needles, she imagined that she could hear splashing. It was definitely too loud for a fish. She came to a toe-stubbing halt, thinking how little she looked forward to seeing her first grizzly. She didn't want to add that first to her list of firsts during this momentous week—first volcano, first glacier, first suspension-bridge crossing, first authentic totem poles, and first free-flying bald eagles. This was not the time to meet her first twelve-foot grizzly.

The lake bulged into a small bay on her right. Its surface was half hidden by the trees leaning out from the shore. She heard more splashing. What was it? A bear, if it got the notion, could easily outrun her, but Green Lodge was now within reach, and she could do 440 yards in a hundred seconds if she really had to.

She crept nearer the shore, turning her head to look over her shoulder at the lodge and gauge how far she was from safety.

It was not a bear, however.

It was tawny, all right, like the rug she'd sat upon last night. But it had no fur. Its skin was smooth and wet. In the water, hair slicked back, facing away from her, stood a man. The ripples rose to his shoulder blades; he had wide shoulders.

She knew exactly who it was.

Clothes lay strewn over a sunny rock; she glimpsed them out of the corner of her eye, and crept closer to them.

This took her behind a tree, out of sight. Jeans, shirt, and underclothes. Socks and boots. Right down to the skin, huh? She touched the jeans, which lay in the shade, and found them warm. His silver belt buckle, seen this close up, included a bucking horse and the date "1967."

She understood. It must have been won in a rodeo. Interesting. Not hard to picture Niall Whitethorne as a champion rodeo rider. On TV they were all handsome, rangy men like him.

He was bending and splashing water up into his face. Then he stopped, motionless, though she hadn't made a sound except to draw in a very deep breath. She saw him suddenly straighten up, and then he turned around, twenty feet from shore. She stepped behind the tree again. Running away from a grizzly and running from that particular naked man were prospects both of which gave her goose flesh and palpitations.

No joking remarks she could come up with, no question about water temperature or the depth of this lake would seem appropriate. She peered through fir branches at him as he looked about, sensing her presence, but not seeing her yet.

He was truly magnificently built!

On each shoulder where his corded neck met his collarbones were those scars she'd noticed yesterday after her "breakfast." Rubbed places.

Suddenly she understood. She stared with her lips parted, frowning. The bottom edge of a heavy wooden mask had made those marks.

There was no Elmer Snagg! That rain dancer had been Niall Whitethorne.

It had been Niall beneath that mask, Niall of the deep chest and sharply defined muscles who was now slowly approaching shore.

There was no expression on his face except grim intent-

73

ness of purpose. Tawny and wet, he was as much in harmony with this woodsy, water scene as any grizzly. Still he was advancing, walking against the pull of the water that had now dropped to his slim waist. To reach his pile of clothing he would have to pass by Sara and would see her. She raised a hand to her lips and bit down on her thumb tip, frowning.

She'd seen this same body dancing, and had watched in rapture, obsessed with it. Today, with a face added, and a mind which already intrigued her . . .

He halted with the water up to his sharp hipbones—hipbones and cheekbones angular among the smooth curves and swellings of muscle. He wore the reflecting surface of the lake slung low around his hips. He was still, then started moving toward shore, again.

She stepped quickly into view from behind her tree. Before it was too late. He pretended not to be amazed. He didn't even greet her.

"Come on in," he softly murmured.

He extended a hand toward Sara, a hand dripping water, palm up, beckoning.

She'd wanted to swim, yes, from the moment she found the water was comfortably warm. She swam most mornings in a crowded, chlorinated university pool. But she had no bathing suit.

Maybe Niall didn't either.

Skinny-dipping? was what she almost blurted out, but didn't. He stood there staring at her bare brown legs and well-filled T-shirt, and then he backed away from her. He moved slowly backward in the water as the surface rose up his smooth, tanned abdomen.

Wincing, Sara immediately guessed the reason for the man's retreat. Her face grew warm, and probably as pink as her thighs, rosy from exertion.

74

"Time for breakfast?" she chirped, turning away from him. "It's a terrific place for jogging."

And she jogged away from him toward the lodge without looking back.

This breakfast was served in the dining room by a broad-faced Swedish woman in a yellow bib-front apron. Bettina Lundmark obviously babied Ruth Bell the way Ruth tried to baby Sara—a chain of affection that amused the newcomers.

"You *must* not drink so much coffee, Ruth," the woman told her. "It'll give you high blood pressure and make you restless, come nighttime."

"Pour some for Sara," their hostess muttered. "If you reach my age, Bettina, then you can hand out advice. You're not even halfway there yet."

Niall hadn't taken long to dress and appear for the meal; at least in front of Ruth the unmasked dancer acted like the very personification of cheerful cooperativeness.

"What time you want to go down the mountain, Sara?" he asked, casually adding as an aside to his employer, "She needs to set up her project. Want anything from in town?"

"Pick us up a couple loaves from the bakery, and Bettina wants more mince, I'm sure. And don't forget the post office."

"Righto," he said.

Sara's eyes widened.

The flight to town felt like sliding down a long bannister. Sara wished she had a hang glider, since in one of those she could float to town. Getting back up the mountain, however, would be the problem. Because the valley fog was all burned away by nine, Niall had no trouble finding the harbor and landing—again with a bone-wracking jolt.

"I'll say good-bye to you now, but let me know your schedule," she told him. "Will you want to go back pretty quickly and get to work on the roof?"

"The roof can wait."

He didn't mention the shopping he had to do, but when she got a whiff of fresh-baked bread, she herself headed toward the little frame building; Niall accompanied her there. He bought five loaves of bread and she bought one for herself. The warm, yeasty loaf was so delicious, Sara and Niall devoured half of it immediately. With her mouth stuffed and eyes shining she stuck the rest inside her sweater, between her breasts, to Niall's obvious amusement.

"Lucky bread loaf," he muttered.

Overhearing this, she said to herself in a softer voice than his, "Buster, when you find out that I know you're the rain dancer—"

The tradestore with sunshine pouring in through its windows seemed like a museum, to Sara. Barrels labeled flour and sugar lined one wall, and on the beams hung rolls of barbed wire, chicken wire, and rope. Bolts of fabric, cowboy hats, wheelbarrows, and no-nonsense crockery crowded out the small candystand and the few postcards displayed.

"I want to advertise two four-week jobs," she told the smiling shopkeeper, and paused to compose a succinct job description.

"Yer lookin' fer men to catch salmon for ye?" the big man asked. "This season? That's crazy, if you'll forgive me sayin' so, miss."

Niall, of course, was right behind her. He didn't have to nudge Sara to express his agreement.

"Will you post an announcement in your window?" she asked him. "I'll be happy to pay for the space."

"Pay? No charge, Miss MacFarland. I've got your luggage right back in the storeroom waitin' for you, and I suggest you talk about your jobs on the valley radio. That'll be quicker. Everyone tunes in. And we can announce it tonight in the town cinema before and after the film."

"You can? That would be great!" Sara exclaimed.

"But it won't get her any helpers," said Niall right over her head to the storekeeper.

"Wanna make book on that?" she said roughly, irked by the superior looks exchanged above her head. No one came right out and discussed her height, weight, and appearance, but she knew what men were always thinking. It wasn't the first time in her life she wished she were stout, tall, and ugly.

"I'd drop by the hospital next, Miss MacFarland," said the middle-aged man, who finally told her to call him Al. "The scientific blokes are down there—those of 'em we have. Educated types."

She finished up the lettering of her sign, and pocketed her pen.

SUMMER JOBS!!
TWO STRONG MEN NEEDED
FOR RESEARCH PROJECT INVOLVING SALMON.
$4 AN HOUR
FOR THREE TO FOUR WEEKS.
APPLY TO S. MACFARLAND, GREEN LODGE.

"Well, S," said Niall as they walked out of the store. "You think that initial disguises your sex? Why, by midnight yesterday I bet everyone in town and on the reserve knew your identity. Without," he added, "any help at all from me. I mind my own business."

"And Ruth Bell doesn't. Well, we'll see if any of these big brawny men around here have the guts to help me out.

77

If not, I'll rig up some ropes and pulleys and do it all myself."

He laughed at her, as she'd known he would, and put his warm hand for a moment on her back.

"You're a treat, little Sara. You really are!"

"You're a chauvinist, big Niall," she replied. "I really suspect that you are."

Past the Bank of Commerce and the cinema they strolled, Sara still warmed by her bread. The film for tonight involved cowboys and Indians. She wondered which side Niall would root for, since he apparently could claim membership in both groups.

She stopped by the Royal Canadian Mounted Police office and told them what she planned to do.

"I'd not like to be the person who sent a delicate young lady so far afield to deal with our fish population," an officer told her. "Seems a Canadian could better do it, if you don't mind my saying so. That is, if it has to be done at all, miss."

Hearing her project derided by a dignified, uniformed mountie stung worse than listening to Al's blunt remarks in the store. At least the mountie wore no hat, no red coat, and was mounted only on a swivel chair.

Niall next disappeared into the ramshackle post office, and she followed him in order to establish an address here for herself. Digging a fistful of envelopes out of a pigeon-hole labled GREEN LODGE, he sorted through them, frowning.

"Anything interesting?" she asked, wondering how many surviving relatives Ruth Bell might be able to correspond with. Niall did not reply. He swung away from her, concealing the mail with his body as if it bore some secret significance. She shook her head in perplexity.

"Anything for MacFarland?" she asked the postmaster.

"Not one thing, miss."

"Well, there will be. Poste restante, correct?"

"That is correct, Miss MacFarland."

She wondered if she'd speak as quaintly as these valley dwellers had she lived longer than her fifth year in Vancouver. That was something else Niall didn't know. That she was born a Canadian citizen and became an American —a "Yank" less than a decade ago, when she reached the age when she had to choose her nationality.

"Okay, I'm off to the hospital now," she told Niall.

This time she outdistanced him, and popped into the two-story, pale green building that dwarfed all the other buildings in town. *I just popped in,* she said to herself, amused that the phrases of her childhood were coming back to her. She'd once had a nanny from Victoria who called trucks "lorries," and diapers "nappies," and referred to Mom as "your dear mum."

The nurses—"sisters," she remembered the term— wore drooping caps and rather long skirts, and gathered around her with great interest until a doctor happened by. Then they scattered like hens at the rooster's approach.

"Miss MacFarland! Or is it Ms.?" asked the young man whose sandy moustache and blue eyes were familiar to her from the dances in Nuhauk Hall. He'd danced in a cloak made of bark, not at all the way Niall Whitethorne had danced.

The doctor held on to her hand so tightly that she had to pull her fingers loose.

"I'm Duncan Karnes," he said, modest enough not to call himself Doctor. "Your research certainly sounds interesting. May I be of any assistance?"

She gaped up at him, amazed at the novelty of his approach. No cold water thrown on her for once, or vote of no confidence. She liked this much better. He was pleasant-looking too. Tall, broad-shouldered, blond, with very good teeth when he smiled. She'd never glimpsed Niall's teeth, though she'd once felt them. . . .

"Well, if I can manage to hire some help here," she said. "I don't pretend to be an Olympic weightlifter, you see—"

"Of course not. Do you have sufficient equipment with you? So far away from your home?"

She nodded. "I've come completely equipped," she said before realizing she made herself sound like a new automobile. "I just didn't plan on your local grizzlies."

He passed a hand rather theatrically over his brow, saying, "Grizzlies! The damage those bloody—I mean blasted creatures can do! We've a poor woman on the ward now who was nearly killed a few days ago. Miss MacFarland—"

"Call me Sara, please."

"Sara, what, exactly, is your area of expertise?"

"Miss MacFarland's a physiologist," said a voice from behind her. "She's nearly completed her doctorate in endocrinology."

Niall put his hand on Sara's shoulder until she made a tiny shrug. The hand went away.

"I see," said Dr. Karnes, looking Niall up and down.

Sara's mouth was still open with shock. Even her mom and dad had trouble with tongue-twisters like "endocrinology."

The doctor said, "Have we met before, Mr.—"

"I doubt that we have been properly introduced," said Niall, parodying the other man's formality. "However, as I recall, the last time I saw you you were being threatened with a giant syringe and a stupendous scalpel."

Duncan Karnes blushed so red that Sara felt sorry for him.

"Oh, that," he said. "Just a bit of a frolic."

"For community cohesion," added Sara, in spite of herself.

Niall's lips were twisted, like hers, to hold back laughter. She wondered if Duncan knew this man was the rain dancer. Should she now commend Niall for his own performance Friday night?

She thought not. Let that wait till the next time they were alone together.

"Miss MacFarland, I daresay your training in chemistry exceeds my own," the doctor said.

"Possibly," she said, her brows almost up to her hairline with curiosity.

"Well, I could certainly use a little help."

Niall scowled, but Sara's spirits soared. Here was one man not hesitant to ask for a woman's aid, though medical doctors, in her experience, were the most arrogant of all professionals. They almost had to be to save lives.

"You see, the patient I mentioned, the bear-mauling case, she lost a great deal of blood, and we can't seem to get her stabilized. The small lab in the hospital has run out of test kits for blood chemistries, transport being what it is in this region—"

"You need to know what minerals she lacks?" Sara finished for him. "You want me to jury-rig some sort of mineral assay?"

"That's it exactly! Right on target." He beamed.

"With what?" demanded Niall.

"I've called around, and the only stock of chemicals besides ours is in the Upper School chemistry stockroom. Unfortunately, it's the school holidays."

"Then we'll break in through a window," offered Niall. "That's been done before."

The doctor opened his mouth to object, but Sara said, "If a life is in danger . . ."

"Cardiac irregularities," he said. "She's not a young woman, Roseangela Pine. She's sixty-two, lives on the reserve, has a history of—"

81

"Let's move! Come on, Sara," said Niall. "I'll pinch somebody's car or bike."

"If you would be so kind—"

"Of course," she said, then called back over her shoulder, "Calcium, potassium, sodium, magnesium—any more than that at issue?"

"Those will do quite nicely!"

"Pompous fool!" snapped Niall.

Running alongside him up the road, Sara gasped, "Well, his was certainly the kindest welcome I've heard since I met Ruth Bell!"

CHAPTER EIGHT

She was accustomed to jogging and chatting at the same time, but Sara saved her breath after making that one irresistible observation. Her mind was on the Indian woman mauled by a bear, as chemical formulae passed before her eyes. Calcium, potassium, sodium, magnesium —all were easily and quickly administered intravenously if one knew how much of each the injured woman needed. That was her job.

Back in the middle of town Niall darted into the tradestore, coming back with permission—so he said—to borrow the motorbike that happened to be parked outside. Sara hopped on behind him, and the wind made tears stream from her eyes as the rodeo star took off down the road.

She had to put her head over his shoulder to hear him as he shouted into her ear. "Teacher's meeting us . . . unlock . . . mounties . . ."

"Great!" she shouted.

The chemistry lab in the valley's modern high school

was well equipped. With a teacher standing on one side of her, a mountie on the other, and Niall pacing back and forth when he wasn't elbowing in to check what she was doing, she managed to gather enough reagent bottles, test tubes, and pipettes to do the trick.

Her return trip down the valley to the hospital was made in the mountie's car; Niall had to come back on the motorbike, trailing along in their billowing dust cloud.

All she needed then was enough of Roseangela's serum to run the assays, and a sharp eye for measurements. No chromatography or spectrophotometry in this little lab, but her challenge turned out to be easier than she had thought.

Niall shook his head, not hiding his admiration.

"Very nice, Sara," he said.

Duncan loosened up only enough to shake her hand again, holding it between both of his. She peeked in to see Mrs. Pine, pale, but managing a smile from among a flock of hovering nurses.

"Lab technician's work. Nothing to it," she said, but Dr. Duncan Karnes continued his litany of praise and gratitude, promising to browbeat or bribe someone into helping her with her salmon project. He dragged Sara in to see the hospital matron who agreed to Sara's using one corner of their big kitchen as her lab. She'd have a basin and tap.

"This will do beautifully," Sara exclaimed. There was ample counter space and an electrical outlet for her tiny centrifuge, plus space for all her insulated dry-ice containers. Her serum samples, once frozen, could be whisked to the airstrip right behind the hospital, and from there begin the flight home to Kentucky. Incredibly convenient. She could have hugged herself with joy.

Hugging Niall on the motorbike ride, she'd squashed her bread flat, but it still tasted delicious, and tided her over until lunchtime. The café just beyond the town's credit union and hotel made her think she was back in the Lexington of two decades ago. Its soda fountain had a long mirror behind it, a fancy green and red jukebox was playing, and neatly dressed young people shared soft drinks and hamburgers in all the booths. Men in western hats and boots and women wearing sweaters and polyester slacks perched on stools along the counter.

Only the Players cigarettes on sale told her she was not in the States; that, and the Orange Crush she drank with her hamburger when she was perched on her own high stool.

Niall couldn't join her for lunch because Duncan Karnes, shedding his white coat and chasing into town after her, grabbed the only other empty stool. Niall was forced to stand up to eat or go off by himself.

He chose the latter.

Duncan Karnes, elbows on the counter, leaned confidingly close to Sara.

"Not much cultural life in Chilto Valley, but I do own an excellent stereo, and I brought all my tapes and records when I moved up here. Do you enjoy Beethoven?"

"Umm-hmm," she said. "My tastes run from the Beatles to Beethoven and from Bach to Bacharach."

"Excellent!" he said. "Delightful to have a person of your caliber here, Sara, though it's for such a short while. I'll have to take you up to see the petroglyphs discovered here, stone carvings by early Indians, quite intriguing to archeologists."

"That would be nice, yes."

"There are dances every weekend. Quaint, if a bit rowdy. A sort of country ball that begins at dark, which means nearly eleven o'clock."

"That would make it difficult for me to get home," she said. "I'm staying at Green Lodge."

"What a pity!" he exclaimed, clapping a hand over his forehead. "Ruth Bell would manage to steal away the prettiest, most interesting—"

"You flatter me," she muttered.

"Sara, suppose you plan to stop overnight here in Chilto instead? We three surgeons have two houses furnished us, which include several empty rooms. Couldn't you accomplish more, living closer to your research site?"

"That certainly would be true," she said.

"Done!" he said, beaming. "I'll pop by the house and have Janice make up a bed for you."

"Janice is your wife?"

"Oh, I'm not married! She's our housekeeper. For Dr. Stedkerster and me." He slid off the stool. "Will you forgive me for hastening away? Duty calls."

"I'm grateful for your hospitality," she said. "And the hospital's hospitality as well."

"What a clever play on words," he said, and then departed.

Sara was smiling into her orange drink. Another step toward getting her project under way. Only one thing nagged at the edges of her satisfaction. How friendly must she be to Duncan Karnes in recompense?

By dusk Niall hadn't appeared again. Her big suitcase was installed in Duncan's residence, and Sara had spoken over the radio, offering employment for two strong men. She also wrote a message to be read after the film was shown in the theater, but everyone except Duncan was convinced that no one needed money enough to work for her. People were either comfortably employed in the timber and fishing industries, or they were too elderly, too young, too busy . . .

She swung by the hospital again, saw that Mrs. Pine was fortified with the proper IV solution, and that Duncan was busy patching up hurt children and automobile drivers who managed to crack up cars on the mere twenty miles of roads in the valley. She'd finished setting up her equipment in the hospital's large stainless-steel kitchen. Any number of men had volunteered to transport her trunks of supplies there from the tradestore, accepting neither pay nor tips. Custom demands that men lug heavy burdens for women. Custom does not, however, demand that men accept a woman employer.

"Sara? I've had the devil of a time catching up to you! What mischief are you involved in by now?"

His voice came from right behind her in the blue dusk. She hadn't heard Niall's moccasined approach.

"Time to fly home, Sara," he said. "You gave me the slip; I've been searching all over for you."

"I've been trying to find you, too, to say Dr. Karnes is furnishing me a bed tonight so I can get started early tomorrow. The hospital donated free space; isn't that grand of them? Tell Ruth I'll move back to the lodge as soon as my work is finished down here in the river. It may not take a week."

He stared at her, clearly disapproving.

"You move fast," he finally said. "And who will you have for hired help?"

"No one. Not yet," she said, resisting the urge to scuff her toe in the gravel like an embarrassed child. "But it's been only one day, Niall—"

"No one is going to do it. Not unprotected."

"I don't want to discuss this further with you," she said sharply. "You get me depressed. Why don't you just fly away home?"

"Want me to dash back down with your toothbrush and nightgown?" he asked. "Or do you have another set of essentials here?"

"I can certainly purchase another toothbrush, Niall.

87

This town seems to have almost everything anyone would need."

"Including a doting doctor who invites you to bed?"

She scowled up at him. "I have the spare bedroom in a house Duncan shares with another surgeon, if it's any of your business!"

"Will dear Duncan also freeze his delicate bottom off in the river, netting salmon for you?"

She turned and marched away from him, not surprised when he caught her by the shoulders and spun her around again.

"Go shingle your roof, Niall!" she exploded. "Fly away home!"

Without checking for possible onlookers, Niall pulled Sara against his hard chest, cupping her head in one hand, and pressing his lips against hers. Both her arms flailing helplessly, she tried to kick him in the ankles, but the wrist across the small of her back was like an iron bar, securing her.

When he came up for air, not lightening his grip, he said, "I doubt that pompous fool who's courting you will get around to kissing you before September."

"Arrogant—" she spluttered. "Arrogant, conceited—"

He let her go.

"We're more alike than you imagine, Sara MacFarland!" he said. "Far better matched than you and that quack. Don't say things you'll regret when you discover that's so."

"I've discovered more about you than you suspect, already, Mr. Whitethorne!"

Because dusk was falling in the valley, and she was standing in his tall shadow, he couldn't see her gaze flit to the now-concealed scars—scars left by the rain dancer's mask. What did he mean, saying they were so much alike? Okay, they both flew airplanes, but he didn't yet know

88

that. Okay, in a sense she enjoyed his macho kisses, but he didn't know that, either, and she wasn't about to let on.

"Go home, Niall. Leave me alone." She shrugged off his hands.

"Make sure you sleep alone, little Sara," he said, not tauntingly, but almost anxiously.

Her eyes widened. Of course she intended to sleep alone, but she wasn't going to tell Niall that. It was none of his business.

Without grabbing her again he bent his head and momentarily pressed his cheek into her curls. "Good night, Sara," he said. "I'll see you tomorrow morning."

She nodded, perplexed and disturbed. Duncan Karnes was easy to read—a lonely, well-educated man in search of a young lady to share his intellectual interests. What Niall Whitethorne really was, she hadn't the slightest notion.

CHAPTER NINE

By ten o'clock the next morning, a plane flew in from the fish-processing plant. It would pick up salmon for Eastern markets after it dropped off her first shipment of dry ice, solid CO_2 at minus 40 degrees. She had brought containers capable of maintaining it at minus 20. Now she was all set.

Duncan Karnes, the hospital matron, and the two older doctors popped in frequently to see how she was arranging her lab. She felt so good working again among syringes and chemicals and shining clean glassware that she had to restrain herself from whistling as she worked. She had her nets, tank, and tags—everything but the salmon and the assistants.

Duncan failed to lure anyone into working for Sara, though he'd talked to his contacts before and after they'd had tea served to them at four P.M. Duncan's lodgings had a little marble fireplace half the size of the stone hearth at Green Lodge. His housekeeper two hours later fed them roast beef and potatoes and freshly shelled green peas from her garden. Janice Cone also brought in a cabbage for Sara to admire—one that would almost fill a bushel basket; she boasted of the gigantic vegetables grown in this warm, wet, fertile valley, as well as their spectacular begonias and roses.

"I know," Sara said, "It's like a little paradise!"

Sara couldn't have been more comfortable in her temporary lodgings with her gentlemanly host, but how could she get her project off the ground with no assistants? It had been two days since she'd advertised for help and as yet she hadn't gotten a single applicant.

From the tradestore to the mounted police headquarters, from the local priest to the blacksmith and the baker, she found that everyone knew everything about her, wished her well, but predicted disaster.

Before noon she bumped into Niall.

What was he doing down here when Ruth's roof needed him? He stood in her path, fists on his hips, an eyebrow cocked, tall and lithe and stunningly attractive, saying, "Well, how's it going?"

"It's not going anywhere, and I'm sure you already know that."

For the first time a suspicion of sabotage came into her mind. How much was this man capable of?

"You have got to hire an armed guard, as I told you, Sara, or the whole thing is over before it starts."

"And who, may I ask—" she began, unable to forget the feel of his hands on her shoulders, his grip as he cupped her head, the fierce, hot impact of his mouth upon hers. "Unh-uh," she murmured, "not—"

"You couldn't *afford* to hire *me*, so don't ask."

"What? Couldn't afford—" she squeaked, disarmed by amazement. "You? Who said I'd ever consider—"

"I was guiding bear hunters when I was fourteen years old, Sara. There's nobody else around here who'd do it, but it would cost you money. Your institute, rather. A lot."

91

"How much?" she asked, aware of his cleverness. Playing hard to get, he was drawing her into his game. She had to know how much he'd charge. Not that she'd have to hire him.

"Seventy bucks a day, as you Yanks would put it."

"I can't afford that!"

"That's what I said. So what do you do?"

She stared into the nearest flowerbed, one of dozens that brightened Chilto's simple white frame houses with reds, pinks, purples, and golds.

"I presume you *are* applying for the job, Niall?"

"But you can't afford me."

"I can't afford to quit and go home!" she cried, and then bit her lip. He didn't sneer or laugh. His grin died, and she imagined he even looked compassionate. The wry expression quickly returned, however.

"Can you come up with the money?"

"Is Ruth Bell paying you that much? She hired you first. I can't take you away from—"

"Anybody can repair her roof. And no, she's not paying me that kind of money. That's not dangerous work."

"Okay. Drop by the hospital in an hour's time, and I'll be able to tell you my decision."

"What're you going to do?"

"Telephone to Kentucky."

Her director at the institute was not pleased.

"Look, Sara, that's a lot of money you're asking for," he said. "We've some discretionary funds, yes, but—"

"Do you want to waste all the money spent to fly me and my equipment up here, Dr. Walters? Look, I'm saving the foundation a lot by getting room and board free. People up here are very generous. It's just that the assistants I'll need won't work for me unless I hire a bear hunter—"

"Run that by me again, Sara. A bear hunter?"

"A grizzly-bear hunter. The waterways are full of grizzlies. They want salmon as much as we do, and won't listen to reason, so I've been told. They maul people. An old woman was mauled only last Saturday. The only eligible bear hunter wants seventy bucks a day."

Sara listened to three thousand miles of silence.

"Well," her director finally said, "I guess if I were shooting grizzlies, I'd charge something in that range myself."

"Call it an error in planning," she told him. "Mine. Salmon mean grizzlies north of the border, but all I pictured were Smoky Mountain black bears. You can slap those across the rump to scare them away from your hot dogs."

"Ummm," he said, still pondering. He wasn't a bad boss. He was elderly, but not by a long shot a notable chauvinist. He was just a little too grandfatherly.

"You'll have the money, Sara," he said. "Just give me the name of the local bank, and I'll get it wired to you immediately. But no more emergencies, you hear?"

"I hear. No more emergencies. I'll keep my nose clean and out of trouble."

"Take the time to get some good color slides too," he added. "Edythe and I have always longed to see British Columbia."

Sara found Niall Whitethorne in the café and beckoned to him from the door. Every head in the place turned when he jumped up from his table to join her on the sidewalk outside.

"I have a feeling I'll regret this, Niall, but you're hired."

"Not so fast, Sara!" he said, raising both hands as if she held a pistol on him. "I make the rules if I work with you."

"With you"—not "for you"—she noted.

"What rules?" she asked warily. "Your ignorance of what this project entails means you can't be the boss—"

He interrupted her again. "Sara, just listen for once. If I risk my neck protecting you, I get a veto over the sites chosen. No wading on blind curves in the streams, where we can't see what's coming. Nobody gets there before me or leaves after I leave. Going to and from the streams, you, at least, will have an escort at all times. Me."

She sighed and headed in the general direction of the hospital with Niall close beside her. "Okay. Okay, that sounds reasonable. And I won't need you for the first stage, down in the river. I *know* the bears don't fish that close to town."

"If you want me on the streams in the mountains, you get me on the river as well. Hire one less man. I'll net the salmon for you."

She shrugged. "If it's okay with Ruth Bell."

"Okay with Ruth? She beat on my door this morning and told me to get my tail down here to baby-sit you."

That wasn't tactful, and both of them knew it, but Sara had her mind on things other than her delicate sensibilities. "I need another man," she said.

Niall's wide mouth curved up at one corner. "For the salmon work?" he teased. "By the way, how did your young quack behave last night?"

"Like a perfect gentleman," she said. "He keeps his hands to himself and treats me like a good friend, which is just—"

"Grand?" Niall laughed. "Have you got him fooled!"

"What do you mean?"

"A passionate, beautiful woman like you, and I'll bet the lad just showed you his photo album and invited you to play cribbage with him."

"He did not! We drank tea and listened to Beethoven,

94

and then he showed me slides of Ontario, where he grew up."

Niall's amused expression almost made her break into giggles. She gave him a little shove. "Go find me a good workman, Niall. If you can't, you are herewith fired!"

"Just try to fire me, Sara," he said in a low, caressing voice that made her back away and put an arm defensively across her breasts. The image of him dancing on stage in the wooden mask came back again just the way it did every night before she fell asleep. She'd have to stop imagining him like that, she thought. Here she was, hiring Niall when she'd sworn she wouldn't, and trying to view him as a platonic friend, an employee. She'd better get in the habit of doing just that.

She didn't expect to get any work done that day, but Niall was a magician. One word from him, and a volunteer for her job came right out of the woodwork or out of the forests, wherever he'd been hiding from her.

Niall brought to Sara a square, fortyish man who looked like a weightlifter. Duncan had pointed out to her earlier that the Indians on this reserve had always been canoe-rowers and fish-eaters—industrious, peaceful people tending to broad shoulders and short stature, while plains Indians hunted game and grew tall, supple, and slim.

Niall would make a good plains Indian. Or son of a tall, pale Irishman.

Mr. Scales—Perry Scales—shook her hand somberly, and spoke with locked teeth on an intake of breath, as so many of his peers did. "Pleased to meet you, Miss Mac-Farland."

"It's Sara. And Perry. Okay?"

Perry grinned. "Quite okay. Now, let's get to work."

She went to the tradestore and purchased a blue-dyed net like those used as fencing on the reserve. Perry carried a twenty-gallon plastic tank on his shoulder, and lugging her case of supplies for sampling, she came along behind Niall, who carried the large net. Again she felt like singing. Things were working out. She didn't hate having Niall around at all. Duncan was sweet, but there was never a dull moment around Niall. She pictured him carrying his big-game rifle, and that image excited her immensely.

While the men in their rubber waist-high waders stretched the seine net upriver from her least favorite bridge, Sara measured TMS—tricane methane sulfanate—into the twenty-gallon holding tank. A .01 percent solution would immobilize the big salmon.

Behind her Niall and Perry were wading slowly in a circle, bringing up the net until the ends met, enclosing an area of river and crowding the fish inside against the bank. Their nonchalance proved their experience with this sort of harvest.

Perry secured the net while Niall, muttering about the cold, climbed half out of the water, and began scooping salmon into her tank with a hand net.

"Only three or four of them," she cautioned.

"Okay, now what do you do to the poor things?" he asked.

"I wait till they'll let me lift them."

"*You* lift them? Not bloody likely, Sara!"

She hung over the tank with her own scoop net, watching the beautiful Coho swim in circles more and more slowly. Niall, out of the water, was close beside her now, leaning over, his shoulder touching hers. She concentrated on the fish to forget the pleasure of that physical contact.

Duncan Karnes only once took the opportunity to touch her arm, and he might as well have been her own brother, for all the impression it made on her. As for Niall, that was a completely different story. Duncan's like all the boys back home, she thought. Niall is a novelty. Unique. A well-spoken forest dweller, a drifter.

The salmon sufficiently distracted her. She swooped her hand net under the smallest of the four, lifted, and got it suspended half out of the water. Bracing the net handle under her arm, she gripped the slippery tail in one hand, and manipulated the syringe with the other.

"Pretty classy moves, Sara," said Niall, "but let me give you a hand."

"I don't need—"

But the fish was slipping, so she didn't make a foolish fuss. A person of either sex would need three hands to manage this alone. Out of the water the fish weighed at least thirty pounds, and this one was the smallest.

In the five cc. syringe she took two cc.'s of blood from the caudal vein and ran it into a tube that she capped and stuck away. Before Niall released the fish, she applied a four-inch spaghetti tag to the muscle in front of the dorsal fin. The fluorescent green tag was, like the test tube, numbered *1*.

"Soon, we'll meet again, baby . . ." she softly sang to the salmon, but Niall overheard, and didn't miss the humor.

"You'll certainly recognize this fish again, Sara. I only hope that decoration won't interfere with his love-life."

"It won't," she said blithely.

"Not pink tags for the girls and blue for the boys?"

"Don't be silly! Here," she said, taking the net from Niall and staggering with the fish down the bank to Perry, "please ventilate this fish for me. Hold him in the water, moving him back and forth, back and forth. That'll force water through his gills; he'll wake up faster. Then let him go free."

Before taking a sample from the second salmon, she glanced at Niall. Admiration shone in his eyes; he wasn't trying to hide it.

Faster and faster they worked, anesthetizing four fish at a time. Niall moved from river to tank, using upper-body strength that Sara would never have even if she took up weightlifting. Then he went back down for more salmon. She wielded an accurate needle, not hurting the fish at all, tagged them, and then it was Perry's job to revive them.

A little crowd gathered around, bare-legged, quiet boys and girls in T-shirts, watching in fascination. Sara smiled as she explained her work, realizing that only for these first days would children be welcome at their research site. Niall would run them off farther upstream, and for good reason.

Compared to Perry, Niall was a chatterbox. Wordlessly, Perry swiftly did exactly as she asked; by the time the sun dropped behind the mountains, she figured he deserved more than she'd advertised as a daily wage. Niall agreed. They discussed this quietly as they tipped out the anesthetic-laced water and rolled up the net. She carried the precious collection of test tubes against her soaked shirt as they walked back to the town, pleased at how much the three of them had accomplished.

"I'll be holding a rifle later on," said Niall while Perry emphatically nodded. "You'll need to hire one more man."

"I can do," Perry said.

"Thanks for your enthusiasm," Sara said, and bade the man good-night.

"Fly home with me tonight," said Niall.

"Huh?"

Perry had crossed the bridge to the reserve, and they'd arrived at her lab long after the dinner dishes had been washed in the hospital kitchen. Niall moved his hand disturbingly over her tired back, massaging it.

"Fly with me, Sara."

98

"I must centrifuge the samples and freeze the serum," she said.

"That won't take a minute."

"How do you know?" she asked him over her shoulder. But she did move more rapidly, fitting test tubes into the angled holes of a shiny steel centrifuge no bigger than an inverted mixing bowl.

She flipped on the motor and set the timer, spinning all the cells to the bottoms of the tubes by centrifugal force. The clear golden serum, frozen in dry ice, would precede her to Kentucky for the elaborate radio-immuno assays with radioisotopes. She couldn't try to explain all *that* to Niall. Bright as he was, there must be some limit to his interest and his capacity for absorbing arcane knowledge.

The setting sun was sluicing a gold wash over all the roofs in town, and gilding the tips of the evergreens. She stood outside the hospital, drawing in deep breaths of incredibly sweet air, wondering where the mosquitoes were, and nodding good-night to bald eagles soaring on six-foot wingspans.

"We want you up to the lodge, Sara."

He was persistent. He closed his hand over her shoulder again, which weakened her resolve.

She was about to say no. Duncan Karnes and Janice Cone were expecting her for dinner tonight, and she had to get an early start in the morning. Then she realized she couldn't very well start without Niall, and he was not sleeping in town.

"Well, I'd better stop by and tell Duncan I'm not—"

"Let him worry. If he hadn't left his post to play the fool at the dances Saturday night, Mrs. Pine wouldn't have needed you to rescue her. No—to rescue her doctor."

"Not necessarily, Niall."

He took hold of her arm. "We fly right now, or not at

all. And I am certainly not welcome at Dr. Karnes's house."

"I don't see why not," she lied. Duncan more than once had spoken slightingly of Niall, though he never gave a reason for his disdain. "Your friend, Tarzan," he called Niall, and Sara had said, "I don't appreciate your terminology, Duncan."

She climbed into Ruth's seaplane, and Niall lost not a moment getting aloft, up out of the dusk into sunlight reflected off the distant snow packs. When he slammed the plane down on the lake, Ruth was in view, waiting on the dock for them.

"Do you always make such a hard landing?" Sara asked.

"Try it yourself sometime. Water's harder than cement," he said.

Before she could say that she would indeed enjoy a stint at the wheel of this plane, he insisted upon lifting her down from the cockpit onto the dock. His hands under her arms, he pressed his wrists against the sides of her breasts and didn't quickly let go.

She was a little giddy by the time Ruth embraced her, exclaiming, "We missed you, Sara! Don't you run away like that! Janice Cone can't cook like Bettina!"

"She's so dedicated to her research," Niall explained, "she wanted to start at dawn. You should have seen this little thing wrestle big salmon. She could almost do without me."

"She must *not* do without you," the old woman commanded, giving Sara's arm a hard shake. "I've never had chick nor child, but now it seems almost like I've got two children . . . or grandchildren, if you must. I won't have my littlest one getting herself drowned or mauled."

"I'll be fine," said Sara.

"I'll keep her safe," said Niall, and looped a long arm around her to prove it.

Ruth Bell beamed. Niall tightened his embrace.

Sara again felt the pleasant melting sensation in her lower abdomen, and the weakness of the sinews behind her knees. She didn't glance up into his sculpted, brown face.

She didn't quite dare.

CHAPTER TEN

Niall couldn't force himself to go to bed. At two in the morning he was still tossing twigs onto the dying fire, sustaining it. When the flames were gone he'd have only cold ashes to stare at.

It was no good that a grown man could think of nothing but one tiny female Yank. One might as well chew a mouthful of delicious food and be forbidden to swallow it, as kiss Sara MacFarland and then watch her march right off to bed. Alone.

He'd kissed her Sunday evening, and then again on the main road of Chilto, and she'd liked it. He was sure of that. She fought him, pretending to be offended, not realizing how the pupils of her eyes dilated with desire and the pulse leaped in the pale curve of her neck.

His own bone-melting passion he could deal with, if only he hadn't got himself so entangled, so enthralled. To think she'd begun as only a soft little kitten to tumble between his hands! The woman he found himself working with was far more than any kitten!

The standard grizzly hunter's hundred-dollar wage he'd

discounted by thirty percent, but he couldn't tell Sara that. She'd say he was patronizing her. He couldn't offer to help her for nothing, or she'd never listen to a word he said. Only costly things have value. If her director had refused to fork over the money, then what? The sight of the tenacious, resourceful little thing biting her lip in frustration had put a knot in his stomach. He wanted to hold her, to shield her, to carry her to his bed, and then to make violent love to her.

When she found out what he was, she'd be livid. He'd better make sure she never suspected. He'd give her a hand, admire her from a decent distance, watch that idiot at the hospital slide into her affections, and then straight into her bed. . . .

Niall, sitting on the grizzly pelt, crossed his arms, elbows on knees, and rubbed his forehead against his wrist. One fire died on the hearth while another flared even hotter inside him. He wanted her. Why not stoke Sara's own fire into a blaze, consume himself in her and then let her go? Forget her entirely.

Too late for that. Sara was more than a beautiful woman. That he could handle—would give several years off his life to handle, hold, caress, and tame. Her intelligence was his problem. Sparring with her was delicious. She was up front and honest, had a temper, a heart, and a mind.

But Sara would return to Kentucky in three and a half weeks, probably to a man as dull as Duncan Karnes. To her, Niall Whitethorne was a novelty, a thrill giver—how often he'd seen her try to conceal her shivers!

It was best to play it the way he'd begun. He'd be far more successful than if the truth came out.

Niall groaned. The ironies of his own past only made this maddening muddle more confusing. It almost seemed that fate was playing a gigantic game with him, making him deceive Sara, who was probably still lusting for the body of "Elmer Snagg."

It was all happening once again. Another lonely valley dweller, and another Yank breezing into town, to sweep . . . The idea of a hundred-pound girl sweeping a six-foot man off his feet amused Niall only momentarily. His wry grin fading, he pictured in her place a handsome Californian, wealthy, divorced, his rifle in the crook of his arm, intent on hunting, just as Sara was so single-minded about her salmon. That was Ian Mulderig. Then he saw a young Indian woman, probably wearing moccasins just like his— vintage 1952. Opposites attract. Does the great hunter go about his own business? No, the Indian woman gets a few years' dose of Los Angeles smog and a little son before the sadness and the tears begin.

The trouble was, he and Sara were not opposites, though she didn't suspect it. He'd almost let a truth or two slip out, yesterday, but bit his tongue. It was his alien image that attracted her. Lose that, and he'd lose her right away. Keep that image, and he'd lose her in mid-September.

"Why'd you ever have to meet up with Ruth Bell?"

Groaning, he asked this question aloud of Sara, who was sleeping peacefully. Upstairs, she was dreaming of fish spawning, not of men and women meshing and melding, thrashing about in frenzied abandon.

He buried the fire's last embers in soft ashes, switched off the light, and with shoulders hunched he climbed the steep stairs to his bedroom, one slow step at a time.

Sara slid out of her bed before six A.M., frowning, cheated of sleep that she needed. Another day handling salmon, and she'd be groggy by noon. Blast Niall! He was upping the pressure, though he'd halfway promised not to. Not to what? Court her? That terminology seemed right for Duncan, not Niall. If only some other woman lived here, to draw his attention away.

No, that would be even worse, she realized. Could she be jealous? Could she want him all to herself when she wasn't supposed to want him at all? Of course that was it, but she must not have him. He was off limits, untouchable. She had to keep reminding herself of that.

"Well, let him keep his hands off *me!*" she grumbled, and had to chuckle humorlessly at her hypocrisy. He must know that she liked him. She asked him enough questions, which he managed never to answer. He'd pulled her half into his lap last night by the fire after Ruth had gone up to bed. He'd kissed her as she'd never been kissed before, and murmured in her ear the things he wanted to do to . . . with . . . for her.

To struggle out of Niall's arms was one of the hardest tasks Sara had ever accomplished, because she was fighting not only him but herself. It was as if nature itself drew them together. Nature prospered from hybrid vigor, got fresh new strength from the spawning of opposites, and she and Niall certainly were opposites.

Niall had said as much himself last evening, joking about feeling like Paul Bunyan kissing Dr. Marie Curie. She said that was a bit outdated. "How about Jane Goodall, the woman scientist who studied the chimps, and—"

Sara tried to take back those words even before Niall's quick response: "I suppose that makes *me* an ape?"

"Not at all!" she exclaimed.

"Then I ought to act like one, huh?" he'd said, falling upon her with frightening ferocity.

Reluctantly, she stopped him and fled upstairs to bed before she could give in to her own desires.

Jogging was an absolute must this morning. That was the only way to wake up, drive Niall out of her thoughts, and cheer herself. Three laps around the lake would make her produce enough endorphins for a healthy, free, self-made high.

Just as she'd done on Monday morning, she stretched briefly, pushing against the tree nearest the lodge. She checked her watch—six ten—and started jogging.

She did not look for Niall. She didn't want to see him. Not at all. Not . . . at . . . all. At least that's what she kept telling herself.

On the third lap, feeling far better, her lungs filled, her scalp tingling, she took a detour by the little bay. He surely wouldn't be swimming—or as Canadians call it, "bathing" *this* early, on *this* morning, would he?

He was.

She felt as if she'd experienced all this before, at the instant she glimpsed that tanned, bare back—the man's marvelously intricate musculature—as he turned around in waist-deep water to stare at her.

As before, she stopped dead-still and returned his gaze. As before, he studied her bare legs and arms, his nostrils flaring, his tense abdomen drawing in. As before, he extended a hand to her without saying anything, inviting her to come into the water. Come to him.

As before, she would make a quip, turn away from him, and flee—but that's not quite the way it happened.

Sara MacFarland, as if mesmerized, turned her back to him only long enough to pull off her T-shirt and slip her shorts down over her legs, staggering first on one foot and then the other. She looked down at her bra and her wispy bikini panties and decided to hold a little of herself in reserve.

But when Sara turned around to face Niall she saw him suck in his breath. Not much was left to his imagination, even while she was still relatively dry.

She tiptoed into the water, down the pebbled shore that hurt the soles of her bare feet and made her fling her arms out for balance like a bird's wings. She felt as if the two skimpy garments she wore were disintegrating under his gaze. He approached to aid her, revealing a tiny black bathing suit, half the size of the suit he had worn when he did the rain dance.

She blinked. Her feet found soft sand, she saw the bottom of the lake sloping away before her, and she dived.

Swimming underwater through chilly crystal until her breath was all gone, she came up treading water, tossing hair off her brow. Her curls had coalesced into a dark, close-fitting cap. She wasn't alone for long. Niall swam out to her and circled. She could see the bottom far below her kicking feet as Niall came in for a closer look.

"Niall—"

"What?"

"The water's great," she said, ad-libbing.

"You sure did a better job of undressing just now than you did the other night."

"Of course. I'm finally myself."

"And what is yourself? Must one only look today, or may one also touch?"

For a reply Sara snapped her body horizontal again, swam strongly away from him, and headed for the middle of the lake before she remembered there was no raft floating there, no platform to rest on. He caught up to her, and she was less surprised than angered to feel a strong hand close around her ankle. She'd grown up with brothers, and holidays at lakeside cabins meant being endlessly ducked and doused. She kicked, couldn't break free, and began to have trouble keeping her head above water. She couldn't go anywhere.

"Hey! Quit that, mister!"

"Stop play-acting, Sara."

"Who's the one who's play-acting?" she spluttered, and managed to kick him hard in the neck so he had to release her ankle. "You were the rain dancer. In that mask. Admit it."

"And you enjoyed watching the rain dance. Very much."

"You could see out of the mask then?"

"Sure." He was grinning, treading water beside her.

"Then you snuck down afterward and sat right behind us."

"Yeah, I 'snuck,' " he said, imitating her accent. "I'd always wondered how women talk about men behind their backs. When a man turns a woman on."

"Who says?"

"You said. To Ruth."

"Who is Elmer Snagg?" she asked, to divert him.

"A kid who got cold feet at the last moment. Lucky for me that he did, right?"

"I wouldn't know."

Suddenly Niall's fingertip slid under the band of her bra in back; he snapped it against her like a rubber band.

"Hey, quit that."

"Convince me, Sara."

"You bully!" She shouted the words, not meaning them. But how did she really feel about him? She couldn't look away from his face or his body. This was idiocy, but she kept up her refrain: "Back off, Niall."

"Sara, we want the same thing."

"I don't."

"Yes, you do. From the first, you did."

"Go away and leave me be."

"Be what?"

She stayed afloat, upright, her hands swirling at her sides and her feet fluttering. She couldn't keep this up forever. If only he'd leave.

Then Niall dove. He left her hanging at the surface, watching him swim underwater, his body dappled with

108

sun through the rippling surface. This was better than his dancing onstage. Then he'd been above her, in one spot, but now he was beside her, behind her, and diving beneath her. Two dimensions became three . . . almost four. He rolled over and over in the transparent greenness, twisting like a seal at play, or an affectionate dolphin. His body brushed against her feet, her arms, until she gathered herself closer together—and sank. She had to tread water or swim, but when she swam away, he swam right beneath her, seldom coming up for air.

When he shot to the surface, his black hair plastered itself against his skull. When he dove again, it softened; it brushed her leg like a scarf of silk.

He didn't touch her except in passing, like a sea mammal. He was such a treat for her eyes that she watched him, entranced, no longer thinking of escape. The lake basin was his amphitheater; she stared down into it, her chin underwater. Once she lost track of him, and before she could revolve in place to find him again, Niall surfaced very slowly, his body sliding against her, his chest touching her thighs, her bottom, her back. Brushing his legs against hers, he lost contact and swam away.

This, she told herself wonderingly, *is seduction.*

Niall almost didn't seem human. He spoke too well to be only what he appeared to be—roofer, rain dancer, rodeo rider.

"Stop intellectualizing, Sara," he said. "Listen to your feelings."

She whirled in the water, but he was submerged again, swimming facedown this time. Wide in the shoulders, narrow in the hips, perfectly proportioned and constructed, he was a marvel of animal architecture. He rolled over languorously, squinting up at her, and she knew how she looked to him, dangling against the sun with no visible means of support, a headless fluttering of four limbs. How he looked to her was another matter. She tried to deal with that. The submerged part of her was as willing as Niall was. From the neck down, she was, in fact, eager.

Niall's hand moved lightly over her back. Unlike Sara, he didn't need both arms to stay afloat. Up in the sun that began to scorch her face, her mind kept working on her problem, trying to decide what to do. *It sure is hard to keep a cool head,* she said to herself.

"Water-wings," Niall remarked, bursting to the surface and looking down at her. "Lovely ones, Sunny. I think I'll nickname you Sunny."

Then Niall made his move. He pulled her to him. As he took her lips, he wound his legs about hers. They both sank slowly beneath the surface.

She was holding him around the neck just to keep from drowning. Mouth to mouth, her waist locked against his, her back sharply arched as she made an arc with him, and they continued sinking through the clear water.

Sara's lungs were empty.

She writhed in panic for breath, and he pulled her swiftly upward and pushed through the surface with her, where she gasped, open-mouthed. He kept both hands cinched around her waist.

"Half drown you and then give you mouth-to-mouth resuscitation all day," he murmured. "I could do that."

She was remembering that his shoulders and neck felt like pulsing velvet under her fingers, incredibly smooth. She paddled to keep afloat, longing to feel that texture again in her hands.

"Get out of these silly bits of lingerie," he said, supporting her in the water with a finger hooked under the elastic of her panties in back.

"No," she said, wriggling to get free.

"You know it's far more tantalizing to be dressed like this than if you were in the buff."

110

"I'm not about to—"

"I'll help."

"No, you won't!"

"You love this, Sunny."

"I am out here to do my work, not to—It's late. I must—"

"You left your watch back on shore. It isn't seven A.M. yet, by the sun."

She didn't miss the contrast in their means of telling time. The vast differences between them made an affair with him seem foolish. But if they had no future together, might she not indulge herself for once?

"You think too much, Sara," he said, as if he read her thoughts. "Trust your body."

That might be it, Sara admitted to herself, but could she really trust herself or this man, in this pristine setting, far from Kentucky?

"I want you, Sunny," Niall said. "Swim over here with me."

He rolled onto his back and slid beneath her body; she linked her hands around his neck as he swam an easy backstroke toward shore. She dipped her head against his shoulder, her lips near one scar where the mask had torn his flesh. It was so comfortable to lie upon his beating heart, to feel protected, safe . . . as well as enormously excited.

He parted the tall, golden grasses growing out into this part of the lake and drew her with him into the shallows where he could sit upon the bottom, half submerged. The grasses shut them in like a basket. She felt his thumbs hook the sides of her panties, pulling downward. Still floating above him, she wriggled to help him dispense with the garment.

Out of sight of anyone on the lake or on shore, she put her lips to his wide mouth. The bra was suddenly gone. He

111

was expert at kissing. He devoured her mouth with a confidence that led her tongue to pursue his when it retreated. She drew his lower lip into her mouth; their teeth touched. She gripped Niall's shoulders, stroking their wet, silken curves, and ran her palms down the valley of his spine. She could see him dancing, swimming, dancing, swimming, even as she held him, and as he explored her body.

How she wished she dared love this man as well as desire him and satisfy his unceasing desire for her. Her workman, her bear guard, who spoke so well, clearly far more intelligent than he wished to seem. "Making love" is the name for this rapture, and love was welling up inside her, filling all her veins, making her want to close his eyes with kisses, draw him into herself, and give him exquisite joy.

If only he felt the same for her.

Niall groaned low in his throat. He held her so close that it hurt, but it hurt wonderfully. He slid her up his body to bury his face between breasts bobbing in and out of the water.

When he freed one hand to tug at his own bathing suit, she said, "I'm not—" without breath to finish the warning.

Instantly he understood, and left his swimsuit where it was.

"Nor I," he said. "I didn't expect company today. Some things can wait. You cannot."

The sun was blindingly brilliant in Sara's eyes. She lay back until her hair and ears were underwater. Niall was all over her, his hands, lips, face nuzzling her, and she went limp under the onslaught. No man had ever touched her so sensuously before.

When she raised her own hands to pass them again over his face, neck, and chest, he seized and kissed the palm of each hand; the sensation knifed into her depths. Neither

112

spoke again. They bit down gently on each other's shoulders; they delicately tasted each other's closed eyelids.

She guessed how much it cost him to treat her so gently, to restrain himself, but reason deserted her at the end and she gave herself over to his erotic caresses.

Her legs kicked spasmodically, and in the still of the dawn Sara cried out, open-mouthed. Waves of pleasure coursed through her body. She held Niall tight as her torso and limbs were rocked in paroxysms of delight.

Niall murmured against her temple. "Is this what you had in mind, my dear?" He pulled her up to sit on his lap again, stroking her. "Next time," he said, "it will be done right. Out of the water. Indoors. In a bed. Mine."

"Oh?" she said, suddenly alert to this unexpected but certainly not unfamiliar tone of voice. Niall would speak to her this way? Make rough demands? His grip on her body was resolute.

When he stood up with her, she glimpsed a small concubine carried off by a tall, grim conquerer. The next moment she realized she was held by a mystery man who was capable of giving her more pleasure than she had ever imagined possible.

She had to fight Niall to get loose, to retrieve her lingerie from the grass, where each piece hung like a little blue flag. Niall's face was growing dark and troubled when he came out of the water. Dressing, he turned his back to her. They didn't speak.

Half of her was still soaring. The other half was contemplating their changed relationship as Niall stood there fully clad, staring at her. He gripped her arm above the elbow.

"Ruth doesn't get up till eight or nine. We've time. We'll go to my room. Now."

"Hey," she said, and pulled free of him. He should not

have said that, or looked at her like that, grabbed her as if she were his property, bought and paid for.

"I beg your pardon," she said.

"You heard me." His face was twisting as if he suffered.

"Don't speak to me like that," she whispered, so she would not shout. "Don't ruin a glorious—"

"Ready to get back to work, huh?" he said bitterly. His eyes were full of hunger, almost misery.

"Niall, I'm sorry, but—"

"How do you think you'll get down the mountain today without me to fly you down?"

"You—But—" Was this an ultimatum? "I'll take a horse," she said resolutely.

"Look at me, Sara."

"Whatever happened to 'Sunny'?" she said, trying to lighten his mood.

"You're being damned selfish. 'Slam, bam, thank you, *sir.*'"

"I did neglect to say thank you," she admitted. "Thank you, Niall. You mean very much to me. But don't act as if you suddenly own me."

"In a sense, I do."

"No man does!" she flared. "Another line like that one, and you'll . . . you'll lose any esteem I have for you."

"Until I take my clothes off again."

"Niall!"

She flushed and looked out at the lake, unable to answer him. Romantic flings in romantic places were not supposed to end like this. Why did he act brutish when gentler words would have brought her willingly into his arms . . . tonight. Or tomorrow. When and if she was sure her head was on straight.

"Just a little fling with a savage lover, huh?"

"What?"

"You've been dreaming of it since you got excited watching the rain dance, right?"

Consternation swept over her. "Niall, don't be silly. You're an intelligent man, a very attractive one, and I—" She could say no more. Such passion ought to lead to a lifetime of love. She did not want a brief fling. With anyone. They ought to end it right now and never touch each other again.

Her eyes stung.

Niall whirled away from her and headed back at a trot toward the lake.

Sara tried not to relish the sight of him, the fluid motion of his hips and legs, the erect, perfect posture. His insults stung, but why couldn't a woman love a man and leave him? Men do that all the time to women. Men and women were just alike. Wasn't that what she believed?

Stupid, idiotic squabble. Just forget Niall Whitethorne. Think about salmon instead, cold, sleek . . . spawning . . . breeding . . . sex-maddened kamikaze fish!

"Let yourself be happy for once, Sara," she scolded herself. "Be perfectly happy in this beautiful country—the province of your birth, not seen for twenty-two long years! Be sunny, Sunny!"

She even tried to whistle a tune as she headed back toward Green Lodge, but no sound came forth.

CHAPTER ELEVEN

That breakfast was as painful as her first Green Lodge breakfast had been delightful. Ruth kept talking, looking from Sara to Niall and back, but neither of her young guests would say a word to each other. Sara kept her attention on her sausage and eggs.

Whether she'd go down the mountain this morning in a plane or on a horse, she didn't know. If Niall decided to quit working for her, however, she knew precisely where she'd have to go—straight back to Kentucky, in humiliating disgrace.

She could not, however, force herself to bare her soul to Niall. To let him bare her body had been easier. Easier? Thrillingly rewarding. But to tell him, *I need you, let's be friends, if not lovers,* seemed impossible.

Not because she didn't care for him, but because she very definitely did. Lust, Sara was beginning to discover, is far less complicated than love. She suffered when Niall suffered, even when she was furious at him. Seeing his dark eyes avoid meeting hers gave her worse pain than any she'd ever experienced in her life. Yet they'd met only three and a half days ago! Was it possible to get so deeply involved so quickly? He must be a sorcerer, or maybe the British Columbian scenery addled her brain.

After Bettina's last decorative little broiled tomato was eaten, and the teapot was empty, Niall was on his feet, crumpling his linen napkin and tossing it down beside his empty plate. Sara sat mute, staring up at him.

"Ready?" he said to her.

"Huh?"

"Are you ready to get to work? To fly down the mountain?"

"But I . . . of course I—" she stammered, to the obvious interest of Ruth and the hovering Bettina.

"Just let me run upstairs for my things," she said, nearly knocking over her chair. As if she'd taken another cold plunge in the lake, relief washed over her. Niall wasn't a bit friendly, but he was civil, and he was still working for her. "Thank you," she said to all the spirits of the forest and the skies.

Niall never said much while piloting a plane, and today he was totally silent. The only things she could think of to say, she didn't. This was not the moment to boast about her own pilot's license or to ask to handle the controls. She sat beside him like a person at a funeral, hoping earnestly it wasn't a funeral for her doomed love.

Working alongside Perry, both of them began pretending that nothing was amiss. His play-acting was a comfort, though she knew Niall still resented her stubbornness. No longer did he want to be her sparring partner or even—it seemed—her lover.

He'd never really been an eagle-headed rain dancer either. He was a last-minute stand-in. Now he had to perform this act, to fulfill his promise to work for her. What grieved Sara most was giving up hope of ever knowing him

117

better, knowing who he was, where he came from, and why.

She asked Perry, the first moment Niall was out of earshot, what he knew about her companion, but Perry shook his head and claimed ignorance. At noontime, she was the one who volunteered to jog to the Chilto co-op for bread and cheese for their lunch. In town she asked several people if they knew Niall, without getting one bit of fresh data.

No one knew him, or no one was talking. She suspected the former was true of the townspeople and the latter was true of Indians on the reserve.

Duncan Karnes, walking near the café, spotted Sara and hurried across the roadway.

"Sara! Sara MacFarland! Wherever *were* you last night?"

"Niall wanted me—" She corrected herself. "I mean Ruth Bell wanted me to come back to Green Lodge," she told him. "Hard to disappoint such an old woman. I'm sorry I didn't get word to you and Mrs. Cone, but it was growing too dark to fly."

"I see," he said. "Am I correct that Tarzan himself is now your assistant? How did you manage that?"

"Miracles will happen," she said dryly.

"Will you join me for lunch, Sara?" Irritation lingered in his voice.

"I can't. I'm taking some food down to the river—to feed my workmen," she added, immediately ashamed of the term she used. Perry might be called her workman, but Niall was certainly far more than that, and both of them knew it.

"Sara," Duncan said, "you'd best pop by the post office. I've heard that letters have arrived for you."

"Mail? For me? Already?"

Like a child on Christmas morning, she dashed away

118

from the young surgeon, almost dropping the bread and cheese in her haste.

The postmaster must have seen her coming, for he thrust two letters toward her. He grinned. "In a jolly great hurry for your letters, eh, Miss MacFarland?"

"Yes, thank you."

One envelope was addressed in her father's round backhand, and the other in her brother Ted's scrawl. Ted, married and a father, wrote more letters than all her other brothers put together. Sara was busy reading Mom's half of Dad's letter about the family cat, hay fever, and the stock market, when the postmaster called Sara by name once again.

"The post for Green Lodge. Would you be so kind as to ferry it up the mountain to Mrs. Bell, Miss MacFarland?"

"Yes, certainly," she said, hardly looking up from her mother's scribble. Taking the small bundle, she tucked it under her arm. On her way out of the post office she nearly bumped into the doorframe, and stumbled on the steps, still reading. Ted was okay. The new baby was fine.

Niall and Perry would be hungry, and she was delaying her own work by her dawdling, so she quickly scanned the last paragraphs, folded Ted's letter, and started jogging.

Inadvertently, she dropped the mail for Green Lodge out from under her arm.

Putting her packages down, she gathered up the mail only to freeze in a crouch, three fingers touching one long white envelope. Its return address was the University of Saskatchewan, Saskatoon, and words neatly typed in the very center of the envelope stunned her.

The address: Poste Restante, Chilto, British Columbia, one might expect.

But not the addressee. The name was Dr. Niall J. Whitethorne.

She picked up the letter gingerly, slowly, dangling it between her forefinger and thumb. She glanced guiltily around her. But she was not the one who should feel guilty! Could Niall again be a deceiver, a fraud, wearing mask upon mask? Incredible!

She stuck the letter among the bills and letters for Ruth and blindly trudged along the road.

Dr. Whitethorne?

That must be Niall's father. With the same name. But Niall's father was a bear guide. An Irish bear guide? Was there a second father who was a doctor? Was Niall really Niall junior?

Before she got to her research site on the river, Sara made a difficult decision. She must satisfy her curiosity. Could Niall really be a doctor? A doctor of what?

Shuddering with anticipation, her hands trembling, she drew out that long envelope again and held it up to the sunlight. Under pain of death she'd never open another person's mail, but if any words inside were visible . . .

Some words were indeed readable. The letter mentioned "the School of Veterinary Medicine" and "recent graduate."

Enough! Recent . . . graduate . . . Veterinary . . . Medicine.

"That—that sneaking, lying, humiliating—"

Without thinking, Sara almost balled up the letter in her fist, but stopped herself in time and stuck it back between two letters of Ruth's.

As if she were drowning, she saw the last three days pass before her eyes in full color and stereophonic sound. She remembered every conversation with Niall. Of course he easily grasped her lectures to him on physiology! Of course he could pronounce *endocrinology* and knew how a centrifuge worked!

120

How could he be so cruel as to deceive her? Why not say something the very first evening? Walking across the bridge, admiring the eagles, he could have said, "We're in almost the same field, Sara. I'm a veterinarian."

To Niall, Duncan Karnes of course was a "quack," a people doctor. It must be infuriating to Niall to see how Duncan snubbed and scorned "Tarzan."

Sara stood in the path, uncertain what to do. How could she face Niall, work with him, knowing—but he didn't yet know that she knew.

It was the rain dancer muddle all over again, but this huge fraud made that little deceit look like a child's game.

One thing, she realized, would be prudent. Hiding her groceries under a bush, she turned and ran full tilt back to town, carrying with her only the Saskatchewan letter. Outside the post office she pushed the letter through the mail slot marked CHILTO VALLEY. Let Niall himself pick up this letter, never suspecting she'd seen it.

On Monday, two days ago, Niall hid some of his mail from her. Now she knew why. He feared she might strip him of a far more concealing mask than the rain dancer's. Why on earth would any veterinarian want to be a roofer, a common workman? Amazing. Imagine Dr. Duncan Karnes pumping gas or mowing people's lawns! It was insane, psychotic; but Niall was neither crazy nor stupid.

Then why did he do it?

By the time Sara found her hidden groceries again, she'd figured out the answer. He kept his profession secret to avoid any serious involvement with her. He must assume that she'd eagerly pursue him if she guessed he was a veterinarian. Because he didn't want any more than her body, he kept up this ruse, played the part of a workman.

Well, now that she'd again uncovered a secret of his, what was she going to do about it?

Nothing yet.

She tucked the rest of the Green Lodge mail in her clutch purse, handed Niall the bread and cheese, and reached for her bundle of salmon tags.

"Cut up the cheese, will you?" she suggested. "I've got to get back to work. Ran into people I knew," she explained. "Delayed me."

Instead of inquiring whether one of those people was Duncan, Niall muttered, "We're starving," and obediently took out his knife.

Might as well be a scalpel, she brooded.

He carved slices of cheese for all three of them, sliced the fresh bread, and then poured tea from Ruth Bell's jug into three plastic cups.

All the while Sara kept her face placid, glowering at Niall only when he turned his back. Ages ago, it seemed, at this morning's breakfast, he was the angry one, while she prayed for a reconciliation. Now this man deserved whatever he got.

Sharing her work with a full-fledged veterinarian felt maddeningly different from hiring the services of a bear guard/salmon hoister. How could she bring herself to "explain" her work further to Niall if he asked? How could she bear to play along as if she knew nothing about him?

That night Sara knew she wouldn't be able to sleep. If only they hadn't quarreled at the lake yesterday morning. If only she hadn't picked up the Green Lodge mail. She imagined herself lying nude in Niall's arms tonight, learning more about love, and perhaps inspiring love in his heart to match hers.

At one thirty, Sara climbed down from her high bed, admitting she was never going to doze off. Maybe she could find some book or magazine in the house to try to

122

read herself to sleep. No decent day's work can be done on no sleep at all.

She paused outside Niall's bedroom door, listening, but heard nothing, not even breathing. There was enough moonlight to get down the stairs without falling, and her bare feet made no sound. She halfway hoped that Niall was up, too, and she'd find him raiding the refrigerator. But he wasn't in the kitchen. She'd begun her search for a bookcase when something in the window caught her eye.

Sara whirled about, her long blue gown swirling about her ankles.

A man was at the moonlit window, silhouetted, looking in.

Horror gripped her. The dark head and shoulders rose up, indicating a height taller than any man could be. *He must be standing on a ladder,* she thought. Could he see her in the kitchen, frozen, her eyes bulging?

Then she knew it wasn't a man at all.

The figure dropped out of sight, and she ran quickly— not away from the window, but toward it, slamming it shut.

In the backyard, now on all fours, hunched a furry giant. The hump above his shoulders instantly told her his genus and species.

Ursus horribilis, the grizzly, the monster Niall was defending her against, at seventy dollars a day.

She watched the fearsome beast suddenly sit back on his haunches. She might be watching a huge, tailless squirrel as he picked up one of their garbage cans between his paws. He proceeded calmly and skillfully to upend it, opening his maw and pouring whatever food scraps Bettina discarded that week right down his throat.

Sara found this hilarious. Giggling at the bear, and then breaking into the sweet relief of laughter, she said to herself, *If only Niall were here to enjoy this!*

123

From her secure sanctuary she watched the bear as if she were in a cage and he were outside it. Resting her folded arms on the windowsill, standing on one freezing bare foot at a time, she gazed down at her unexpected visitor. He took his time snacking, and then tossed aside the garbage can, belched mightily, dropped his forepaws onto the ground again, and lumbered out of sight into the forest.

"Bravo!" cried Sara, and found herself applauding.

As she ran back upstairs she was still smiling, still wishing Niall could have seen that. A charming giant having a midnight snack. The thought of Niall raising a heavy, well-oiled big-game rifle to his shoulder and shooting her bear appalled her. Ruth Bell's courageous bear-killing now seemed like homicide.

This time as she passed Niall's room she could hear the unmistakable sound of bedclothes rustling. Had he heard from all the way upstairs her childish burst of applause?

Sara could not resist tapping lightly upon Niall's door. Putting her lips close to the paneling, she whispered, "I've just seen my first grizzly, Niall!"

"Congratulations!" came an answering whisper.

Sara stood perplexed, wondering whether to feel offended or to laugh at his surprisingly quick response. So he wasn't able to sleep either?

Before she decided on her next move the door was shoved open in her face.

"Where's the bear?"

"He's gone," she said. Sara could not see clearly in the dark hallway, but she suspected Niall was wearing nothing at all. "And I couldn't stand to see you shoot him. He was so cute, holding our garbage can like a kid downing a big milkshake!" she added, trying not to think of Niall's nakedness.

To her relief, Niall, the bear hunter, didn't make a dash

downstairs for the rifle that hung on the wall, but just stood over her with moonlight behind him, a blacker shadow in the dimness.

"You think I'm that bloodthirsty, Sara?" he snapped. "I told you my father detested trophy hunters, bear slaughterers. If I ever have to shoot a bear to save your life . . ." And then he stopped.

Sara waited for a moment before murmuring, "You'd rather save any animal than shoot it, wouldn't you?"

"Who wouldn't?" he instantly retorted. "They're an endangered—"

He stopped, and she regretted pushing him so hard.

"Sara—" he said softly, and she held her ground as he moved toward her. She felt rather than saw his fingers reaching out to her, to brush against the curve of her throat. She released her grip on the plunging neckline of her nightgown and leaned her cheek against his warm palm. They stood like that for a long moment, wordlessly.

She did not move, though her gown began to slide down, off her shoulder. He bent, his lips feathering over the flesh now bared to him.

"Niall," she sighed, sliding her arms around his narrow waist. His tremor might have been from the chill of the night or from the shock of her intimate touch. "Are you cold?" she asked him.

"Yes," he said. "You can warm me, Sara."

Yes, she could, and she wanted to do so. She gathered his warm nakedness against the velvety softness of her gown, wanting him, yearning to reveal what she'd discovered about him and end these cruel deceptions. Then she would give herself fully to him.

His hands were now stroking the small of her back, sliding down over the curve of each hip. The slow tenderness of his touch almost moved Sara to tears. She rested her head against his shoulder as they stood suspended in

125

time; neither was able to speak or even knew what words to say. If he drew her into his bedroom, he'd meet no resistance. There was no resistance left in her.

Now Niall bent, and slid an arm beneath her knees and lifted her high against his chest. It felt as lovely as she'd expected, and she looped both arms about his neck.

He did not, however, carry her into his room. He carried her into her own bedroom and placed her gently upon her bed. She didn't release her hold on his neck, pulling his head down to kiss him.

He kissed her—lying half over her, drawing the quilt over his bare back, and then cupping in his hands the breasts he so easily uncovered. His thumbs teased her stiffened nipples while his tongue penetrated deeply into her mouth, tasting, probing, stroking the warm cavern as her breath came gasping into his mouth.

"Niall, oh, Niall," she said, involuntarily arching her back, up, up, until she seemed to rest only on her shoulders and heels.

Her thighs trembled apart as they had never opened for any other man. Just as he tensed to move his body over hers—to merge the exquisitely aching centers of their bodies, she could hold back the words no longer.

"Why do you live a lie?" she asked. Even as she reveled in the joy of his touch, she dreaded his reaction. "Tell me who you are, Niall. Don't make a fool of me."

He arched his back, rising up off her body to prop himself on stiffened arms.

"What . . . are . . . you . . . saying?"

She should have told him. Immediately told him all she'd discovered, but she wanted the truth from him. Already she was begging, lying beneath him and begging him to confide in her.

"What I could tell you would hurt," he said in a voice grown scratchy and rough. "Believe me. Don't ask questions, Sara. Enjoy what we have. What little we can have of this, for only three short weeks."

Three weeks. Love for three weeks? She planted her fists against his chest to push him away.

"Then I don't want you!" she cried. She was lying, of course, and she was close to tears.

"Okay," he said curtly, and slid off the bed, slid off her pulsing body. "Good luck sleeping, Miss MacFarland. Ms. MacFarland, rather. If you change your mind just . . . just whistle."

Her lips by now were too bruised and dry for a whistle; she felt bruised to the soul. As he shut the door behind him tears began to roll from her eyes onto the pillow.

"Niall, Niall," she whispered. "What shall we do?"

CHAPTER TWELVE

Sara found her work more rewarding the following week, up on the mountain. Her emotional life, however, was another story. Perry recruited his nephew to help him, a charming, articulate young man heading for forestry school, and Niall moved a few yards off, to high ground, where he sat scanning the stream banks for grizzlies, a huge, oily-looking rifle resting across his thighs.

"I flew over the streams several times," Niall told Sara, all business now, "checking where grizzlies congregate. We may not see many in the places you work."

But he let her choose the places, within limits. The streams feeding the river were wide and shallow, and filled with smooth, pale stones, among which the female salmon made nests for their eggs. The hooknosed males frantically swam back and forth, spewing milt.

It didn't seem very romantic to Sara. But one didn't think much about love while wading in knee-high boots, searching for brightly tagged salmon.

They seemed to be everywhere—brilliant streamers rippling like banners flying from their dorsal fins, intent on their mating and oblivious to the way she'd decorated them for their starring roles in her project. Sara worked as quickly as possible, tranquilizing, taking samples, and then reviving the fish so they could get back to their deadly serious business—the business of insuring a crop of salmon for next year. This generation would be dead within the week. Soon after they mated, each would die.

"Next year I should sample the steelhead trout, which mate for two or three years," she told Perry's interested young nephew. "This stream, for them, isn't a one-way street. We need to find out why the salmon age quickly and die, but their close relatives live."

After a week of aloofness Niall began to thaw, and Sara was struck by the intensity of her response to him. The first stolen kiss on the nape of her neck didn't make her swing around and hit him; it made tears come into her eyes. She hid the tears, but knew he must suspect her relief and her joy.

Maybe he was married. He could have lied about that too. Had he run off to the forests of his childhood, leaving a wife and little children behind in Saskatoon?

No, she doubted that. Since learning his true profession, she had watched him carefully, seeking his true nature. One evening when they had staggered into Green Lodge and both flopped down in easy chairs, Sara saw Niall use his training.

At first she was too tired to notice anything. Ruth's ancient calico cat was always draping her rag-doll-soft body over everyone's lap. Tonight Jinx chose Niall's lap.

Sara watched out of the corner of her eye as sinewy, brown hands ran over old Jinx's body, not really petting her, definitely examining her. *Ah-ha!* Sara breathed to herself. Proof positive. Niall even rolled back the cat's lips, squinting at Jinx's remaining teeth. He'd probably been doing this all along, when Sara had no reason to take notice. His tenderness moved her. She almost envied the cat.

If I were an injured puppy dog, she brooded, *then I'd get that kind of attention from him.*

Looking over at Niall, she couldn't help feeling horribly embarrassed. She still flushed when she remembered how self-important she must have sounded, lecturing on biology as if Dr. Niall Whitethorne were a high school student. Dr. Whitethorne's patients would be dogs, cats, horses, and cows, so she probably knew more than he about the physiology of Canadian salmon, but still! How humiliating!

Back at Green Lodge, she quizzed Ruth Bell, who conceivably might know something.

"What this valley needs," Sara remarked, "is a good veterinarian, isn't that so? It has doctors and a visiting dentist, but I haven't heard who takes care of people's animals."

Ruth, purveyor of all the valley gossip, agreed wholeheartedly that Chilto Valley could sure use a veterinary surgeon, and went right on carving small figures of fishermen and hunters, which she painted in bright colors for the valley children.

Sara didn't have the heart to pick up the lodge mail from the post office again. She let Niall do that, and he returned with fistfuls of letters for her from home.

Now that her lab had moved to Ruth Bell's kitchen at the lodge, she didn't see much of Duncan. He'd often just happen to be in sight of the airstrip when they landed, and would stroll over to chat. She wondered how he always knew when the seaplane was arriving and leaving. But his presence didn't much interest her.

Then one day Duncan approached Sara again.

"There's a spectacle this weekend you ought not to

130

miss, Sara," he excitedly told her, too soft for Niall to overhear.

Remembering the spectacle of the Indian Dances, she perked right up.

"Oh? What do you mean?"

"The only amateur stampede in the province. Up on the plateau. It's the annual reunion of ranchers from three hundred miles around. Four days of dances and what you'd call a rodeo."

Rodeo? That word certainly crashed like a cymbal in her head.

"Sara, will you fly up there with me in the hospital plane? I must attend the inevitable injured, and your company would be delightful."

She made her decision right on the spot. "I'd be glad to go," she said. "It does sound like fun, and I figure I deserve one day off. I've been numbering tags, dealing with the serum, and recording observations day and night and on weekends too."

"I don't doubt it," he said, sighing. "I've never seen a young woman quite so diligent. You impress me, Sara. Very much."

She stepped backward, away from him, afraid that as Niall disappeared toward the tradestore Duncan might at long last try to embrace her. No prospect could be less exciting.

Moments later it occurred to Sara that Niall might attend this Canadian rodeo. He might even ride. No, she thought, surely he wouldn't! If he were going, he sure hadn't invited her, nor had Ruth Bell mentioned any rodeo.

"Wanna see the event of the summer, Sara?"

She was bent over her dry-ice containers, trying to project whether the next shipment of coolant would last until her departure for Kentucky. She didn't see Niall enter the kitchen, and of course one cannot hear a man approach whose shoes are made of soft deerskin.

"Yes?" she said, already guessing what he was going to say.

"There's a big weekend—"

"The stampede? I'm going with Duncan."

She had no choice but to tell him the truth. Immediately, darkness covered Niall's sharp features. She added, "You never mentioned it, so I thought—"

"You can spare so much time off then? You've had no time even to see a movie or take one more swim in the lake, but you'll give up two days for an outing with—"

"I felt I needed a break," she said lamely, resisting the urge to admit how much she'd prefer spending the day-and-a-half holiday with Niall than with Duncan.

"If—" He stopped himself, turning away. "Anything you need done for tomorrow?" he asked gruffly over his shoulder.

"I was just checking the dry ice. I think one more shipment will last me."

"Sara's life is measured by the melting of ice," Niall remarked on his way out. "When the next batch of dry ice is melted, then she will be gone as well, melting away, forever."

"Melting . . ." she mused, struck by the poetry of his unexpected outburst. She remembered the night of the grizzly bear. Lying in her bed with Niall—completely melted—she would have been his had she not asked that unaskable question: What are you?

What a pity to spend her first days off with Duncan Karnes! For a moment she found it impossible to speak, but when Niall was halfway out the door, she called him back.

"You'll be going to the stampede then?"

132

"I have to fly Ruth up there. She's bent on having a frolic."

"Oh. And there's a dance and a rodeo?"

"There's a dance and a rodeo, yes."

"I see." She dragged one finger across her test tubes, jingling them in their rack. The crystal sound died away. "Well, perhaps we'll meet there?"

"Perhaps we will."

On Saturday morning Sara packed a wicker basket with a change of clothing. Feeling like Little Red Riding Hood headed out on a date with Grandma, she caught a plane ride with Niall down to the valley to meet Duncan Karnes.

They didn't say much to each other, and Niall didn't even get out of the seaplane. After he taxied up to the dock, he lifted a hand in salute. Sara climbed out onto the dock, shut the cockpit door, and watched the seaplane pivot in the blue water and dash back into the sky again.

A pity; she'd leave here without once handling the controls of that plane—without even telling Niall she was a pilot. That was one thing he didn't know about her. Another was that she loved him.

The flight up-valley was breathtaking. Sara pressed her nose against the window of the hospital plane, watching the river grow narrower as they rushed eastward. Sheer mountainsides studded with tall trees converged in an enormous V. A tiny road straggled alongside the river but gave out when it met sheer cliffs.

The plateau town of Bumbry boasted less than fifty roofs, she discovered as they circled and dropped lower. Its lake, however, was crowded with brightly colored seaplanes, and its airstrip with small conventional planes.

"Be prepared for some mosquitoes up here," Duncan

warned. "Some people camp out, but I've reserved a room for you in the hotel. Down the hall from mine."

He took her to the town's one café for dinner, where they sat at the end of a trestle table filled with noisy diners in cowboy hats and boots. They ate not salmon but Dolly Varden trout. Because Duncan was not a scintillating conversationalist, Sara's chief amusement came from the motley bunch of children chasing each other among the tables covered in red checkered oilcloth. Everyone teased the waitresses, wolfed down gigantic dinners, and interrupted each other with news of the past half year.

"Now let's go for a walk. I'm so full I need some exercise," said Sara, eager to see more of the town.

They strolled past corrals full of horses the size of Percherons. She recognized the rodeo ring by its tall, sturdy fence and the four wooden chutes at one end. As they walked they dodged circling automobiles full of people hanging out of the windows, calling to friends. Sara needed no more proof that this was the reunion of the year.

Children skittered everywhere—hiding, seeking, and eternally squealing. On the dry grass trucks were parked among trailers, campers, and wagons for drayhorses. In a grove of trees stood a herd of tents as well as sleeping bags spread right on the ground.

Duncan today was bold enough to keep Sara tucked protectively against his side, resting a hand on her far shoulder, though he said very little. This suited Sara fine, for her mind was on another community hall, another Saturday night, when a half-nude rain dancer first caught her eye . . . and then her mind and heart as well.

Darkness was slow in coming, but finally people began converging on a tin-roofed building. Its capacity was perhaps three hundred, but it looked to Sara as if five hundred people must be cramming themselves into it. She ap-

134

preciated the warmth of the crowd on the chilly evening though. Each dancer must have had only about three square feet of space in which to cavort.

A guitar, two fiddles, and a clangy old piano began playing, while women served coffee out of kettles set on long, sagging tables. Sara, already hungry again, eyed the piles of hot dogs.

But first she wanted to dance. Dancers ranging in age from five to ninety-five spun around the floor in a polka, seldom colliding. Sara squinted down at all the boots that crashed upon the floor boards, many adorned with bright jangling spurs.

Girls with rosy skin, thick, black hair, and fringed and beaded deerskin costumes made Sara feel plain, pedestrian, and citified, even in boots and jeans. At least she fitted in better than Duncan did, in his slacks, polished black oxfords, and gray nylon Windbreaker.

A Royal Canadian Mounted Policeman stood in the doorway laughing with the celebrants. It was disappointing to find none of the RCMP mounted on horses. They all seemed to drive cars.

Wine and beer bottles went rapidly round the noisy, communal gathering. Even the vivid cursing seemed full of fun. Sara nodded and smiled at people who kept nodding and smiling at her.

One Indian woman leaned closer to Sara and commented. "Some folks are born and grow to three, four years old, 'fore they come to Bumbry and see a stranger's face, first time."

Sara knew whose face she longed to see, but her searching gaze was unsuccessful. Duncan didn't notice her wistfulness, and when she asked to dance, he refused. He stood close to her, commenting upon the hopeless task of bringing perfect hygiene and health habits to some of the tribes of the plateau.

Suddenly, a young, freckled cowboy in a hat too large for him asked Sara for a dance—signaled his request, rather, for voices were becoming inaudible in the whooping ruckus.

Sara grinned her assent and plunged into the crowd with him, knowing Duncan disapproved. Duncan disapproved of a lot of things; he'd said this was his second year in the valley, and—he vowed—his last.

Sara tried to stay off her young partner's boots. Boxed in by other dancers, somehow they managed to caper about the room, and when the polka ended, he thanked her very formally, touching his hat brim, swaying a bit.

Her next dance partner enunciated no polite request for a dance, and he certainly did not touch his hat in a gentlemanly salute. As she stood beside Duncan again, shouting some amusing observation up to him, an arm whipped around her waist, and out she flew into the mob of dancers.

"Niall! You're here!"

His eyes narrowed to slits under his arching brows, Niall held her tight against him. Sara did not struggle. She had to dance or be carried bodily. Niall's hand crushed her fingers; his other arm held her tightly as his knees thrust against her legs. Like all other men except Duncan, he wore cowboy garb—heeled boots, jeans, and a western shirt.

Niall danced with his face bent down and pressed against Sara's cheek, not letting her look at him. He danced very well, forcing her to follow his strong lead. As he whirled her dizzyingly, desire rose in Sara, but she felt safe among their five hundred carousing chaperones.

"Where d'you think you're sleeping tonight?" he said into her ear.

"In the hotel. Duncan got me a room."

"With him?"

136

"No, not with him."

"You're staying with me, Sara."

"I am?" she gasped, and asked, "Where?" before half thinking. She was leaving in only a week, and they had no future, even if Niall stopped his game-playing and told her the truth.

"In my tent," he said. He danced her alongside a serving table and scooped up a paper cup of wine. Sara put it wordlessly to her parched lips.

By then Duncan had fought his way over to them through the crowd. He looped an arm around Sara's shoulders.

"I think she's had enough of you," he told Niall.

"What d'you think she is? Your patient?" Niall demanded. "Go tend your sick, quack."

"Hang on to me," Duncan said to Sara. "I'll help you. You don't have to be manhandled by—"

She didn't want to be helped. She bolted the rest of the wine, standing sandwiched between the two tall men so differently dressed, one in denim, one in city-styled clothing. The tumult increasing around them, Sara found herself gasping for air. Niall wasn't embracing her, but his hard length pressed meaningfully against her.

"Move off, Karnes," Niall said, taking hold of Duncan's arm and forcibly dragging it down from Sara's shoulders.

Just as she feared, Duncan tried to regain his grip on her and shove Niall away at the same time, but he lacked the strength and agility. He had to resort to words.

"She's not your type, cowboy!" Duncan shouted. "She's a cultured young lady so far above you—"

"Duncan!" Sara exploded.

". . . practically has her Ph.D. degree, and the idea of you daring to put your dirty hands on—"

She herself might have swung for Duncan's cologne-scented chin, but Niall swung first. Luckily, he had little leeway, or he might have laid the surgeon out on the floor with one blow. Even the people surrounding them seemed to notice nothing, but Sara felt both men's muscles contract, and past her nose Niall sent a quick jab that hit Duncan right across the larynx.

"Let's get outa here, Sara!" Niall hissed, and pulled her with him out of Duncan's reach.

She came along willingly, telling herself, *Forget Saskatoon and secrets, forget questions, common sense, complications. Forget everything except what you both want and deserve.* She wanted this man—Niall Whitethorne. She wanted all of him.

Tonight.

CHAPTER THIRTEEN

Niall surely had the same idea. He swept Sara out of that hot, noisy confusion into the cool blackness of night.

"Your boyfriend will have one helluva time finding you," he exulted. "You're mine tonight, Sara. Like it or not."

She liked it, but didn't admit it. His arm, tight around her waist, indicated that he expected a fight, but she came willingly. Her pulse raced and her breathing quickened with excitement. But when she glanced up at the determined face of her abductor, she read more than lust in his features. He must know this was the end, their last evening together. Love and pity surged up within her—pity for them both.

His tent was set well away from the others, a burned-out fire before the flap door. In the moonlight Sara could see that the tent was shaped like half an egg; a modern tent, no tepee. He unzipped its fabric and netting doors, and she came inside, watching him zip the two of them snugly into his hideaway—sealed and secure.

No, Duncan would never find her. This might be a swan

song, her farewell to Niall, the end of a doomed relationship, but first she'd show him what she felt for him. Sara's eyes began to sting. She wanted to speak of love, but dared not.

The sleeping bag was downy under her knees. Niall crouched beside her, stroking her back, embracing her, lowering her onto the forest bed, where she waited, looking up into darkness.

"Sara," he whispered, asking a wordless question. "Sara?"

"Niall?"

He must hear the catch in her voice. Desire was still there, spiced with fear and wariness, but she felt much more.

"Niall? Do you know—"

"Hush. When we talk, Sara, everything's ruined. For once, let's finish what we started—"

She knew what he meant. Tonight she would not deny him the sensual joy she had discovered that day at the lake.

"Dear little one—" he said on an intake of breath, his fingers busy with the buttons of her shirt. She tried to unfasten the snaps of his shirt, but her hands were too shaky.

He began to kiss her, finding her lips after first tasting her throat, her eyelids, and the tip of her nose. She rubbed her nose against his while her arms rose to loop themselves about his neck, and her fingers explored the dark jungle of Niall's thick hair.

To get her out of her jeans, Niall had to rise to his knees, lifting her feet in the air. Sara's boots and jeans came off together. Her chest rose and fell as if she were running uphill. When she felt his touch again, his chest was bare—warm, smooth and bare.

Niall lowered his body half on top of hers and held

Sara's head between his hands. She sensed him staring into her eyes. He pressed his forehead against hers.

"My little Sara," he said. "Mine for one night."

She didn't care any longer about anything but making love with Niall. Her head fell back against the down-filled bag as he moved his hands firmly along the sides of her neck, over her shoulders, and onto her breasts, quickly freeing them of her bra, then lifting them and pressing them together.

"So firm and beautiful," he murmured.

Her hands, half encircling his waist, told her his body was the same—perfect. Perfect for her.

He lay more heavily upon her, sliding between her trembling thighs, so she could not mistake what would be the end of this tender fondling.

She lay helpless and willing beneath him. Still he held back. He stirred her senses, kissing her lightly, tongue to tongue, velvet to velvet, stroking her with the same rhythm, above and below.

Sara breathed—almost wept—the words, "I love you."

Niall turned to stone, a statue full-length upon her. "Hush!" he said, and smothered any further speech by clamping his hungry mouth upon hers, lashing her tongue with his.

"Niall!" she said, hardly making a sound, and seized his shoulders, pulling him closer. She stroked his long back as she'd done in the water, when he'd taught her . . . denied himself and given her all that she yearned for.

He rolled over with her, so Sara lay straddling him, too weak to move. He slid her body upward, tantalizing each of her already aroused breasts with his tongue. A throbbing heat coursed through her body. She ached with the need to satisfy him, take him into herself and hold him there tightly. She stroked both palms over the planes of his

141

face, and his hands worked their way down her back to close over her tightening buttocks.

He slid her whole body up and down his torso.

"Don't look at me," he commanded. "Don't say anything."

She knew why. He refused to love her as a whole person. He needed only her body to satisfy his thirst; he wanted to leave love out of it. Body to body was enough.

Eager for him, she would follow his lead. He had already played servant to her once. Now they'd be equal, as in a game. It was always a game with Niall. Let him be only what he pretended to be, and she could return to Kentucky, never to see him again.

Never?

That word tore a sob from her throat; feeling it before he heard her gasping tears, Niall embraced her, bringing her head down to rest in the curve of his neck. He patted her back.

"But I *love* you," she persisted. She had to say it, understanding now that she'd never loved any man before. Parting from Niall would be like emotional surgery, cutting him out of her heart. How could she tell him that? He wouldn't show anger or sneer at her love; he'd retreat into his stoic silence and then surely disappear. That was far too much to risk.

Niall suddenly moved. He swung Sara over onto her back again, and lay with all his weight pressing her down. Not breathing, she relished this new sensation of intense pressure. Before she was starved for air, he propped himself on his elbows. She parted her lips again, and he covered them with his, at the same time sliding a hand down her side, to hook his thumb into the elastic of her bikini panties, the last bit of clothing protecting her.

The filmy garment slid down her legs and was gone.

Passion again swept through her body, making her

groan, arch her spine, and stop crying. Niall put his palm over her mouth, bending his head down on her breast, breathing raggedly, perhaps praying she'd say no forbidden words to him.

She lifted her head and kissed the side of his face, her hands urging him closer.

With a sudden groan of purpose, Niall slid both hands under her hips, securing her, and, with a wondering gasp, sank deeply into her.

He felt her soft lips move over his face, lips curving into a smile. Her temples tasted of salt. She was crying.

He found her breasts again, the nipples still firm and uptilted. *Have her and leave her. Be cold, be hard, take Sara and then forget her,* he tried to tell himself, knowing all the time that that would be impossible.

He held himself back, stroking slowly, endlessly within her, meanwhile imagining himself in the morning taking her back to Karnes, that indescribable fool. She couldn't fall in love with Karnes, but she mustn't fall in love with Niall. Love turns so easily to hatred when any woman finds herself deceived. Deceived as to what her lover is—who he is—and she was suspicious already.

He couldn't distract himself any longer. Sara, his precious . . . not his, never to be his, but he'd have this night to remember. Her strong little legs rose and wrapped themselves around his waist; her arms clutched him to her breasts as her breathing came faster and faster. He drove his tongue once more into the sweet hollow of her mouth, matching with its small movements the powerful thrusts of his loins driving harder and quicker.

They finally cried out together, their voices merging, as he drove them both to ecstasy.

Sara expected to weep for the joy of it, but instead she heard herself laughing softly. Would the rippling spasms of her body ever die away? His body was the first part of him she'd discovered, when his face was lost inside a mask. Now she had all of him, loved all of him, and he lay like a dead man upon her, his weight welcome and good. His violence did not hurt her; it only left her satisfied.

When Niall lay beside her, his fingers sliding over her smooth abdomen, she turned her head and kissed him.

"Niall . . ."

"Sara, you are so—"

He didn't remember any woman who'd held him so tightly, inside and out, whose body exulted at his touch the way hers did. Tomorrow there would be no shame, no blame, no recriminations or doubts. He was sure of that. She loved him.

He pitied her for loving him.

He pitied himself for loving her.

"All night," he whispered. "Only this night, Sara. Then we part friends."

He curled in a curve around her, fondling her breasts, waiting for his body to recover. Again and again he'd make love to her, make this little miracle woman happy. He felt uneasy when her breath again came faster, and she turned round in his arms as if in the darkness she could see his face.

In a small, anxious whisper, she said, "Dr. Whitethorne . . ."

He recoiled at her words.

How did she know? How long had she known? Did she come to him with open arms the minute she learned he was good enough for her?

"How did you find out?" he demanded, meaning to move away from her but by reflex locking her body more tightly against his.

She took a while to reply, but she sounded sincere.

"I . . . I saw a letter to you from your university, and

144

. . . I didn't open it—quite—but it was clear you're a . . . you're a doctor of veterinary medicine. And you never told me!"

"You never told me you'd found out!"

"You could have stopped me from lecturing you in biology, Niall! You live an enormous lie."

She tried to sit up, and he let her. He opened his arms and released her.

He forced himself to say, "So now I'm fit to make love to, huh, Sara? Well, it's over and done with. You've had your fun. Go on back to the States and dig in other men's private lives."

She drew in an angry breath; he prayed she would not cry. Maybe *he* would.

"Boy, do you ever play games!" she snapped at him. "Deceit after deceit. And self-deception is another game. Deception must be your middle name."

She was trying to find her clothes. He didn't help her. Instead, he raced her to get dressed.

He won. She was ramming her feet into her boots when he was already standing, bent over in the confines of the low tent. He waited for her to say she hated him. He wanted that word. It would release him.

Instead, she hissed, "Here you sit, wasting your skills, playing cowboy, playing tough guy, when there must be animals suffering and dying all around here. That's selfish. Self-destructive. What are you, some kind of neurotic?"

"Sara, if you knew my reasons for being here, coming back to the valley—"

She interrupted him. "You knew I . . . liked you before I had any notion you were the rain dancer, Niall. Long before I suspected you were called Doctor. I was waiting for you to tell me of your own accord, so there'd be none of this—this awful conflict."

"Sara," he said, weakening. He put his arms around her

struggling body. They fell to their knees on the sleeping bag, and finally she stopped fighting.

"Sara—"

"And I said I loved you."

"I can't say 'I love you' because—"

"Because what?"

"You're going away. In one short week. What future is there for us? If I followed you, think of the exams, the U.S. licensing procedures. . . . Not likely I could ever practice my profession in the States. And if you gave up your work—"

"I wouldn't," she said staunchly.

"I wouldn't respect you if you did. That's just it, Sara. We have to end it now. No talk of love. It can't be. Start forgetting me."

"I can't!" came a wail that tore at his heart.

"Oh, Sara—my Sara," he groaned, holding her in his lap till they toppled over onto his primitive bed. She wept, and he tensed all the muscles in his face to keep back his own tears, halfway succeeding.

"If I asked you to marry me, to work with me—" he began, and was cut short.

"No. No! I won't give up my doctorate to become a veterinarian's assistant. No, Niall. And I won't be a full-time housewife, and I don't want kids right now. Not right now."

"Neither do I."

Again, silence. He feared to kiss her. Of course she couldn't give up her profession at its very outset. The very thing that made Sara wonderful was her mind, her resourceful, tenacious, clever mind. That, and her warm, seeking body.

So this is where love gets you, Niall brooded. Through a burst of delicious delirium into bleak, inexpressible pain.

146

CHAPTER FOURTEEN

The second time they undressed each other they moved slowly, groggy with love and with sorrow. One night. This one night, and then it would be the end.

How many times, all through graduate school, had Sara seen men and women fall in love, delay marriage, hoping against hope. Students met because they specialized in similar fields—population genetics, or invertebrate zoology or limnology, but two appropriate jobs hardly ever opened up at the same time in the same area. One would go off to Boston, the other to L.A., or to other equally distant cities.

The day when a working woman followed her husband everywhere, without one word of complaint, was gone. A teacher, secretary, or nurse could manage to relocate, and if Sara were a physician, a dentist or a lawyer, it might be different, but—

"I was born in Vancouver," she told him. "We left Canada when I was five. All during my childhood I was a Canadian citizen."

"You never told me that!" he exclaimed, pausing as he was unbuckling her belt.

"You never told *me* a lot of things!" There was no longer accusation in her tone, only tender amusement.

"Your being born here wouldn't help us much," he mused, "but you could immigrate to Canada if you had a Canadian husband."

This was the second time he'd mentioned marriage! She searched for a bit more courage to help her say, "Niall, you haven't even mentioned love."

"I haven't?" He cupped her face in his hands. "If I haven't, Sara, please, believe me, that word's been behind my teeth for several weeks now, trying to get out."

"So that's why you talk with your teeth locked," she teased, her heart swelling with sweetest relief.

"I love you. I'm not a man who finds that difficult to say anymore. I love you, Sara. My Sara."

She didn't want to start weeping again, and he didn't sound very steady himself.

"What are we going to do, Niall?"

He said nothing, only lay beside her, caressing her face, curling her curls round his fingers.

"My mother," he said, "married a Yank hunter, a man a lot older than she. He took her to Los Angeles, but she couldn't survive there. She got desperately depressed and ill. Psychosomatic, probably. When I was three she came back here with me. The divorce was congenial, and he visited me a couple of times—my father did, before he remarried. A few years ago he died. My step-father is one of the best men I know. He gave me his name, of course— Whitethorne."

"What was your real father's name?" she finally was able to ask him.

"Mulderig. As Irish as the Blarney Stone."

She saw all the parallels; he didn't have to point them out to her.

She said, "In Vancouver, perhaps I could find a position."

Niall groaned aloud.

"What's the matter, Niall?"

"Sara, I came back to the valley because it's the only place on earth I want to be. I couldn't take any more city life. Those years—"

His abrupt silence would convince anyone before he finished his statement.

"The cars and the billboards, the racket and the smog—"

"I know. If I weren't going back to a small city like Lexington, I'd feel sick at heart. But Kentucky is green, with big trees . . . well, saplings compared to trees out here, but—"

"I've got good jobs offered me in Saskatoon and in Edmonton, Sara. Good positions, with high pay. Downtown, right in the cities. They're waiting for my decision, and time's running out."

"In vet clinics?"

"Yes, but that's not what I want. I took an extra year of studies, Sara. I strengthened my background in wildlife medicine—bear, wolves, all species of deer. I aimed to be traveling, doing wildlife work much like yours, tagging animals, testing them. I'm finished with dogs and cats; even, I think, with horses and cattle. But a wildlife position hasn't come open yet. There aren't that many."

"How did you survive so many years in school in Saskatoon?"

"I fixed up an old bus to live in, and parked it under the biggest grove of trees I could find."

She smiled ruefully. His longings seemed so right for him, fitting so well her first image of the bronze rain

149

dancer, the swimmer, the soft-hearted hunter. She hugged him appreciatively before grasping what all of this meant.

Only a city fit her; only the forests fit him, no matter which country they lived in.

They made love to each other one more time. It was the only thing they could do.

Afterward they lay exhausted on the sleeping bag and Sara's mind began to race. How could anyone, man or woman, slave all year round for seven years past college graduation and then give up everything for a rose-covered cabin . . . or tent, in the midst of the Canadian wilderness? What about her own chosen career?

The bitter irony was that she loved—she almost worshipped this awesome Canadian wilderness. She'd give up city life without a whimper if she would still be able to work.

What would they do to survive? Yet how could they survive without each other?

She wasn't accustomed to sleeping with anyone, and though she wound all four limbs around him like a koala bear gripping a tree, her sleep was restless and plagued by nightmares.

The worst dream put her into an airplane, soaring over a narrow, winding Kentucky highway. Down below, she spotted a yellow school bus, and somehow she knew Niall was at the wheel. Ahead, around a curve, she could see two cars approaching, racing, filling both lanes. She dipped lower, to warn him, waggled her wings, screamed out of the cockpit, "Stop Niall! Danger! Stop, stop, STOP!"

"Stop what, darling?" he said, shaking her a little to awaken her. "It's only a bad dream."

The next dream was little better, and the dawn of rodeo day found her groggy and stiff, and, like Niall, sadly depressed.

"I want to go take a look at the horses," he said.

They kissed before and after he shaved. In the cool freshness Sara held the mirror for him, watching the razor's swift strokes.

Sunlight was glimmering through thin columns of blue campfire smoke. Everyone around seemed to be frying bacon or boiling coffee over wood fires, and everything smelled delicious, including the tangy smoke.

Sara's thoughts, however, kept returning to destruction and death—relics of her nightmares. Like Romeo and Juliet, their love was doomed from the start. Right this minute dying seemed preferable to losing Niall. Dying, yes. Giving up all that she'd worked and fought for, no. She shook her head at him as he shrugged into a fresh blue and gray plaid shirt. No words seemed necessary.

"I love you," he said, and was gone.

She located his tin trunk of foodstuffs, found bread, bacon, and eggs, and collected some twigs. There were short logs stacked by the tent, and she played Girl Scout with relish, in an attempt to occupy her mind. She made a small fire and began cooking bacon and eggs in a skillet.

"So here you are!"

She took her time looking up. No good having her bacon burn.

"Yep. Here I am."

Duncan didn't say anything more, so Sara did.

"I'm sorry he had to hit you last night, but you asked for it. Someday you'll find out why. I'm flying home with Niall this evening, Duncan. I hope you enjoy the stampede, and not too many riders get injured."

"I'm sorry for you, Sara MacFarland," he said. "I didn't think you would really . . . ever—"

"Don't say any more!" she half shouted. "Just go away. Go to . . . heal someone. I don't want to get angry again."

He went away. She made herself coffee and sat cross-legged in front of their tent, eating right from the skillet. The meal, strongly flavored with wood smoke, was the best breakfast she'd made in a long, long time. Sara's thoughts returned to the previous night and her eyes welled up with tears. No. She had to be strong. She wasn't old yet. Maybe love could wait. They'd somehow spend their last twenty years together, somewhere, someday in the far-distant future.

At noon the rodeo hadn't yet started, and Niall came back for her to take her sight-seeing.

"I'm of two minds about this rodeo," he explained. "Half the events are examples of what cowboys do every day for their living. The rest is daredevil theatrics. The horses sure don't like the bucking strap, but it's on very briefly, and they get paid in hay and oats. It's not like bullfighting. . . ."

She loved to see him exhibit his veterinarian's concern now that his secret was told. She listened intently, walking with him hand in hand.

"You rode here as a boy, didn't you?"

"It was the joy of my life. Even then I didn't like spurs though. I just wanted to win. Ride any beast and win prizes."

"I believe it. I saw your silver belt buckle."

"Won many of those, and some gold ones," he murmured softly, and then changed the subject. "Never saw any chap as furious as Duncan this morning."

"Tough luck," she retorted. "I just hope he doesn't mix up his medicines—"

"And give tetanus shots to drunks," Niall added, grinning. "You didn't tell him what I am?"

"I figured you deserved that honor," she said. "When you're ready."

"I'm just sick of all the accolades," said Niall. "People

152

treat you differently if you're called 'Doctor.' Either it's the old cliché about being a credit to my race—"

"Which is half Irish," she murmured.

". . . or people get jealous, resentful. 'He's too good for us, anymore,' they'll say. Hard to prevent that."

"Except by repairing people's roofs and catching salmon."

"Exactly. While I try to decide between Edmonton and Saskatoon or just being a tramp until the right job comes along."

"Stay out of the field long, and you'll fall behind."

"I know it. There's no library with veterinary journals in the woods." He looked down at her, squeezing her hand. "And no way you could finish your degree. Dr. MacFarland."

"Ph.D.s don't often use their titles. I'd get mistaken for an M.D. and be asked to cure somebody."

"Niall! Sara!" came a familiar raspy voice.

They looked down at Ruth Bell, all decked out in a ten-gallon hat, a red western shirt with white piping, and jeans. Her boots were high-heeled and dazzlingly shiny.

"I wondered where you were, Ruth," Sara said.

"And I've no doubt where you two have been. Well, go to it! You're only young once."

Niall let out a burst of laughter, and Sara fought a blush, as she said, "Wrong, Ruth. You've been young for eighty-four years."

"Wrong, Sara!" she said, merrily swaying, her cheeks very pink. "I acted like the dowager queen till my old man died. *Then* I got younger."

The loudspeaker over the rodeo arena had been noisy for some time, welcoming visitors, cracking jokes, naming cowboys who'd ride in the events, and advertising "the only bar between Japan and Bumbry." Lost children were

153

paged, a doctor was summoned, and every rancher got teased with in-jokes Sara didn't begin to understand.

Ruth trotted away, not quite in a straight line, but plenty of people stepped forward to greet her, passing her from one to the other, so she hardly needed to be steady on her feet. Sara shook her head in amused amazement.

When the rodeo events began, Niall lifted her up to sit atop the dizzyingly high fence, saying, "Hold on tight; it'll sway under you."

It did. Everyone climbed the fence or stood on the rails, looking over the top, and the fence vibrated. Her perch faced the chutes, giving her a wonderful view. Niall kept on moving, greeting old friends, squinting into the pens of calves, bulls, and horses.

There were many events: barrel races with classes for men, women, and little girls, wrangling, pair-roping, the cutting of cattle, stake-racing, bronco-busting, and wild-cow riding, with a saddle on the cow and three men per cow to control her. Sara enjoyed the wild-cow milking—into a beer bottle.

Calves, running loose, careened around the arena, and a clown diverted them with skilled gymnastics. First came the roping and cutting events, full of whoops, cheers, and flying lariats. As a sort of intermission, small boys ran a foot race with a thirty-pound salmon as prize.

Sara spotted Niall perched atop the fence opposite her, right up against the chutes. He up-ended a bottle, drinking deeply, and passed it to another man in a cowboy hat like his. She felt proud of him but slightly concerned too. Would he get drunk? He deserved to, maybe, but if his courage soared, and he attempted to ride—

As in her nightmares, she said to herself, *Niall, stop! Danger, Niall!* In his frame of mind . . .

Now he was leaning over the chute, checking the bridle

on a bronco that another man gingerly mounted. The door flew open, and the ride commenced.

Tall horses rose, straight-legged, between her and the sun, their riders' boots flying out sideways. A twist and a jerk, and off came the cowboy, landing neatly on the back of his neck. Just when you thought he was dead, up he bounced, hands clasped above his head.

Limping cowboys received sedation out of long-necked bottles brought to them right on the field of competition. Sara could sense Niall's frustration over being back after so long, having been such a champion here in his youth. Their eyes met, and he lifted a hand in salute.

One horse went on strike. It kept all four legs as stiff as those of a rocking horse. The rider sat there grimly while the crowd roared with laughter.

Rider after rider rose up into the sun on bronco or Brahma. Sara admitted that she'd never watched anything more exciting. Her blood churned; flying hooves churned up the dried mud of the rodeo ring.

Niall was not where he'd been sitting. Before she could get her hand to her lips, eyes widening, she saw him settle into the saddle of a bronco. "Oh, no, Niall! Not you, Niall. You'll be injured!"

His palomino came out of the chute flying. Niall had no saddle and wore no spurs. One arm straight up in the air, the other hand knotted into a rope around his mount's belly, he rose up with the big horse, crashed down, flew up, and spun around. She glimpsed a flash of red in the crowd—Ruth Bell, waving and shouting. Then the bell sounded.

Effortlessly, Niall slid down the side of the horse, and swaggered a bit as he strode over to the fence where Sara sat.

"Just one ride," he promised before she could speak. "Just one, to see if I can still do it."

She smelled liquor on his breath.

"Oh, please, Niall. You're too valuable—"

"And too old?"

She reached down for him, but he had to find a lower section of the fence to climb out of the arena. He didn't come to her again, but went back to the chutes.

Dared she tag after him, play nagging wife when she had no right to do so? Should she beg him not to ride, though he'd ridden one bronc so successfully?

Sara stayed where he'd put her and raged deep inside. This was boys' sport, blood sport, no place for a trained veterinarian to play cowboy.

More Brahma bulls were fed into the chutes, barely fitting into the wooden boxes, and bull riders mounted with the greatest of caution. Niall stayed very close by, hanging over the nearest chute, gesturing, pointing, reaching down to fix ropes and straps. When would he yield to temptation again?

Sara felt ill. If he rode, she didn't want to see it. She'd cover her face like a coward, even though he'd be riding for her. To prove to her something he'd already proved many times over—that he was everything she'd ever wanted.

Sara stared at a giant white Brahma now being mounted in the chute. A slim cowboy in blue slid onto its back, and immediately the beast reared. The crowd gasped. Still in the chute, the thing reared up. Niall, perched on top of the chute, ducked out of the way. No one was laughing anymore. Hooves pounded wood. Sara heard herself scream, and then everyone screamed.

The Brahma went over on its back. In the chute. On top of its rider.

She heard the young fellow scream. And keep on screaming.

Niall moved fast. Braced by his legs which were spread

156

on top of the chute, he gripped the bull's halter, pulling straight upward, cursing the bull. The cowboy, out of sight below, shrieked again. Men wrenched the chute gate open to reveal the struggling bull's whole side. Only one arm and one leg of the rider were visible.

"It's killing him!" Sara screamed. "Get it off him!"

Everyone else screamed the same words. Men flocked around the chute.

Niall had vanished.

"Niall! Niall!" Sara uselessly shouted.

The bull was unmovable. Men tried to turn it sideways as it sat, to drag it out through the gate.

Then she saw Niall, saw his head, at least, as he stood in the chute, down behind the bull's gigantic bulk. He was hoisting, his hat off, his face darkening with effort. Men hung over the top of the chute, reaching down.

"Get out of there, Niall!" she screamed behind the fist pressed against her teeth.

The limp rider, dragged upward, hung between Niall and the bull, handed from the one man to many men, and then he was safe . . . and then the bull began to right itself.

"Niall! Look out!"

Niall disappeared. Shouting began again. One man freed and maybe still alive, and another man in the chute out of sight as the bull heaved, snorting and struggling to get all four legs under its bulk.

The bull came lunging out through the gate, straight toward Sara, across the arena. She wasn't the only spectator to slide down the split-rail fence before the furious bull struck it, rattling its whole length. The clown ran to catch hold of the bull's tail, digging his heels in, being dragged. Horsemen appeared and herded the bull toward the wide arena gate into a pen.

Sara fell to her knees, got up, and ran for the chutes, not trying to see anything past tall spectators or through the high fence. Stumbling, fighting hysteria, she shoved right and left, her throat locked on one name.

"Niall?"

The bull's rider had vanished. Three men were carrying Niall out of the chute into the arena, shouting, "Surgeon? Where's the surgeon?"

She clambered between two widely spaced rails to reach Niall, forcing her way close enough to put her hands on his still face. No man challenged her, and one answered her unspoken question.

"Got squashed a bit, miss. Kicked, maybe. Brave chap, ain't he?"

"Will he be all right?" she asked, not expecting an answer. She just had to say it. Then she added, "Niall? Can you hear me?"

Vaguely she heard the announcer saying the words "Whitethorne" and "Chilto" and "injured . . . courageous—"

When she was about to drop to her knees beside Niall, do anything she could to breathe life into him, he opened his eyes.

"Where's the bull?" he gasped, wide-eyed.

"It's gone, mate. You did well. You saved that poor chappie the bull sat upon!"

"Niall, are you—?" gasped Sara.

"Sure. Just got the wind knocked out of me. That's all." And Niall, with a little aid, got up.

He staggered. Sara threw her arm about his waist and made him lean on her. The crowd cheered. Niall paused to lock his hands together over his head, and then he limped out of the arena, leaning heavily on Sara.

"At least you're alive. You risked your life," she muttered, giddy with gratitude.

"Somebody had to, Sara. The poor kid wouldn't have made it."

"How'd you get him out from under the bull?"

"I didn't. I moved the bull over. A vet knows how. Even a Brahma has a sensitive spot or two."

"Duncan better check you over."

"He has a badly hurt patient. Let's go see that poor chap. As for me, I'm okay. Besides, he's not my favorite doctor."

"You may have internal injuries, Niall."

"Nope. Nothing a shot of whiskey won't ease, or a massage by Sara." He grinned down at her.

They pushed through the crowd around Duncan, who was already sliding a needle into the young cowboy's shoulder.

"What's his prognosis?" Niall asked Duncan.

Duncan sent him a scathing look. "Well enough. Don't block out the light. Get back, there. I need some more room."

"Need any help?" asked Niall.

"From you, Niall?" he snorted. "Not bloody likely."

"You didn't see who saved this chap's life?" demanded one of the onlookers.

"Niall saved him!" Sara snapped. "And he happens to be a—"

"Let's go, Sara," Niall said angrily. "The boy's getting his color back. He'll survive. In spite of this quack."

She dragged Niall away before he had time to finish. Duncan needed his composure. His patient required a lot of doctoring.

The moment they were out of the crowd she pulled Niall's head down and kissed him. Niall staggered again.

"You're hurt, Niall. You've got to get care—"

"I'm a doctor, too, remember? I can prescribe for myself, and right now I prescribe a little rest in my tent. I need to be put to bed with a sweet nurse. Almost a doctor."

"I think that means me," she said.

159

CHAPTER FIFTEEN

"You can't fly the plane home, Niall."

She was getting tired of repeating that line.

"Sure I can. After a little more doctoring."

She helped him out of his shirt and his jeans.

"Remember when you had to help *me* undress, one night," she kidded him, and got a quick kiss for a reply.

In Niall's tent—its flaps drawn back for light—she carefully examined every inch of her lover. Bruises were forming everywhere, though he insisted he wasn't in pain. Instead of whiskey, she kept giving him kisses.

"I love you, Niall. When you vanished, when I thought you'd been crushed to death under that bull—"

"You were unhappy?" He grinned into her solemn face.

"Unhappy? I was sick! I understand now how Victorian ladies used to faint. I wish I could have fainted—missed the most awful moments of my life, waiting to see if you—"

He became serious now. "I think you do love me."

"I do."

"And I love you." Moving rather stiffly, he embraced her.

"It would solve your problem, though, if I did get my brains knocked out. Then you could go back to Kentucky without any—"

"You hush!" She kissed him into silence. "Lie back and rest. You got very little sleep last night."

"And neither did you, my lover."

After he'd had a nap, with her lying wakefully beside him, Niall's muscles stopped twitching. He managed to haul himself to his feet, and Sara helped him get dressed.

"I can walk. I'm all right," he insisted. "Let's head right back to Chilto now."

"Well, I've sure had my holiday," said Sara, glad that Niall didn't feel like toasting any more old friends with whiskey or feasting on barbecue.

"Ruth will stay the whole weekend," Niall told her. "I can fly back up to get her."

She contemplated the way he walked and realized it wasn't very steady. He rubbed his face and also the back of his skull, wincing.

"Niall? Are you sure you haven't got a concussion?"

"Ah, now Sara plays medical doctor?"

"Be quiet, and listen to me. After a close call like that, you'd better have Duncan look you over. Really. I'm serious, Niall."

"Trust his Hippocratic Oath that he'll treat me without bias? He's not my best friend."

She nodded. "He'll be nice, or I'll murder him with my two hands."

But Niall refused to present himself to Duncan Karnes as a patient. He packed his tent, picked up her suitcase from the hotel lobby, and loaded their things into Ruth's Beech 18 float plane.

"You gonna fly home with me, or fly to Chilto with Duncan on his next ambulance-run?" Niall asked her.

"I'd prefer flying with you," she told him. "If something happens, my license *is* current."

"Huh? License? A lot of good a driver's license will do you—"

"A pilot's license. Single-engine. One hundred and three hours flying time. I've had a little experience in a twin, but only with an instructor."

He cocked an eyebrow at her. "Will wonders never cease! Another secret out, Sara."

He gave her a hug. "Come on. I left a message for Ruth. Let's get home. I don't—"

"You aren't feeling very well."

"Let a half-ton Brahma lean on *you,* and see how you feel!"

"That's what I'm talking about, Niall. To take a plane up, when you're possibly injured—"

"You'd rather fly in the hospital plane?"

"No! But you ought to."

"Not a chance. Come along, Sara, if you trust me."

She didn't trust his judgment, but she went along, climbing into the cockpit behind him. This time she examined all the controls closely. "Tell me about those and those," she said, pointing.

"Oil shutters and cowl flaps," he told her, losing no time turning on the fuel pumps and fuel selectors. She could follow all that. She stared at the paired levers for propeller pitch, mixtures, and the paired throttles. It was a touchy business flying a twin-engine plane. If everything's not carefully equalized, there's the danger of a spin.

"The velocity of minimum control is seventy-six knots," he told her. "I lift the nose at a hundred knots."

Fastening her shoulder harness, she asked, "What altitude are we flying at?"

"About ninety-five hundred feet. It's two hundred miles home. Any more questions?"

"Nope." She felt squelched, but no less concerned. As he taxied out onto the lake, she looked back, hunting for Ruth, Duncan, any familiar form. Soon she had a good view of the rodeo arena and the dance hall from above. As Niall banked sharply left, she saw only sky.

It was some comfort that a twin had a redundancy of systems. If one engine went out, they could still make it home. She couldn't shake the remnants of her nightmare. That, combined with her terror over Niall and the bull, kept her frightened and on edge.

"Tell me how to land this thing."

"Keep the approach speed below the flap speed, but too fast is better than too slow," he told her. "Point your nose where you want to land. Pitch for glide path, and power for air speed."

She hoped she understood his concise explanations. He didn't talk while he flew, and all her chatter must be distracting him, Sara thought. She sat back in her seat and watched him intently as he operated the controls.

A few minutes later Niall's head slowly nodded forward. He slumped in his shoulder harness, lower, lower, almost onto the yoke.

"Niall! That is *not* one bit funny!" she snapped.

He didn't move; he just hung there, both hands palm up, limp in his lap.

"Okay, okay! You've given me a scare. I won't worry about any more catastrophes, so sit up. Hey, sit up, Niall. This plane needs you!"

No movement, no sound, no teasing retort.

She reached over and roughly shoved him. "Niall, you quit it!" her voice rose an octave.

The plane banked, and his body swayed like that of a hanged man.

"Niall!" The word was a scream now.

Twisting toward him, she gently lifted up his right eyelid. She brought her free hand close to his eye. The muscles around his eye would jerk when he blinked.

She did it again.

Niall did not blink.

"Oh, Lord. Oh, Lord!"

There was nobody to hear her say "I told you so," so she didn't.

What had Niall said about the blasted oil shutters and cowl flaps? She'd have to ignore all that. The wing flaps worried her. Those were for landing. *What's the maximum flap speed? Look on the air-speed indicator, Sara,* she told herself. *The top of the white line.*

Her eyes frantically scanned the maze of switches. It was like a big computer board, but with almost everything paired. Two engines. She detested twin-engine planes, and as for float planes . . .

But dials were labeled. U meant undercarriage, or wheels. No sweat, the floats were always down. One awful worry canceled.

She could see Chilto in the distance now, down the sweeping valley. What was the approach speed? She'd try eighty knots. She pulled the throttles back to slow the plane, and brought the nose up.

Keep approach speed below flap speed; he'd told her that.

"Niall? Please, wake up. I can't land this thing!"

She jostled him again, anger suddenly turning to dread. He might be dying. From a burst blood vessel in his brain? A stroke? A hematoma? They might both die if she couldn't get them down. She remembered Niall's bone-jarring landings, and *he* was an expert. Water is a harder deck than cement, he once said.

Don't think about that. Think about numbers.

She added a little throttle, watching the air-speed indicator. What was the stall speed? Her feet danced on the rudder pedals.

She didn't want to circle and give herself time to worry about landing. There was plenty of fuel, but she might go into a panic. If she snatched up Niall's headset, no one in town could likely guide her in better than she could herself, in spite of her lack of experience.

What did Niall do before landing? She'd watched him often enough. Twins landed three times faster than singles. The harbor zoomed toward her; she eased the nose down. The biggest building in town was the hospital; she wanted to head straight for that.

". . . coming in too high and too fast!" she squeaked, and then bared her teeth.

When the floats hit the water, deceleration was immediate and spectacular—like plowing through sand. She clung to the yoke, aiming for the beach beside the hospital. The airstrip was beyond that. No houses, no trees to take wings off. Better to slew sideways, over on a wing, she told herself. Anything but standing the plane on its nose.

Which is exactly what she did. Neatly and slowly the nose went down, the tail rose, and she and Niall ended both hanging facedown, like rag dolls.

She had little time to contemplate further disaster. People must have seen and heard her come roaring in, even without any radioed distress call. She was right. Within moments hands wrenched open both cockpit doors. Tied up helplessly in her harness, she almost cried with gratitude.

She started talking at once, croaking words.

"Get Niall to the hospital. He's comatose. Needs help. No, I'm fine. Let go of me; tend to him."

Niall still didn't move.

"Hey," she called to him as he was taken out of the

harness and then out of the plane, "I didn't land this thing just to have you go and *die* on me!"

She didn't even look at the man and woman who steadied her and dabbed at whatever was running down her neck into her shirt.

"Niall, you wake up, you hear?"

"Get her to hospital too," a voice said, and Sara suddenly wasn't standing any longer. She was horizontal, with a stretcher under her. They wouldn't let her sit up. Niall was gone from the area already.

"All right, all right, Miss MacFarland. Your friend's headed for hospital ahead of you. Calm yourself. You'll both be all right."

"Are you sure?" she said, blinking away something flowing into her left eye. A man dabbed at it, wincing. Nothing hurt; she felt fine. What about Niall?

In the hospital doorway she tried to sit up again, but hands pushed her down. She started to scold and struggle, but then suddenly night fell like a shroud, and Sara didn't get anything said at all.

CHAPTER SIXTEEN

"Well, Sara, *I* made myself famous by killing a grizzly with a twenty-two-caliber rifle. You've found another way to get the valley's attention!"

Ruth Bell, standing by Sara's hospital bed, jerked open the white curtains around the bed. Ruth pointed.

Sara sat up and gasped.

"Gave you a room with a ruddy good view, wouldn't you say?"

Through the tall window of the hospital ward Sara could see the mountains, the blue harbor, the airstrip, and—smack in the middle of that pleasant landscape—a crowd surrounding what was unmistakably the tail of an airplane sticking straight up in the air.

"Oh, no!" Sara groaned.

"Oh, yes!" The lined, pixie face nodded. "Got every soul in town out to see my airplane, you did."

"I'm sorry, Ruth."

"Sorry about what? Saving your own life and Niall's? Niall would never make a landing like that. I suspect that *you* were the one who brought the ruddy plane in."

"Where's Niall? How's Niall?"

Sara whipped back the covers and swung her legs out of bed.

"He's fine, child. Just you lie back. You've lost a lot of blood."

"But if you only 'suspect' I landed the plane, that means Niall's not conscious and talking yet."

She stared at Ruth. "What blood?"

"The plane's side window shattered. Sprayed you with bits of glass."

Sara felt her neck and found one gauze pad taped right under her ear and another bandage among the curls on her head.

"Oh," she said, again attempting to rise. "I want to see Niall. I have to see him."

"I think you're in love with that crazy cowboy."

Sara's groaning sigh was answer enough. She planted her bare feet on the cool linoleum floor, and immediately the back of her hospital gown flapped open.

"What's this thing I'm wearing?" she said, reaching back. Women patients in other beds in this ward watched her—mouths open, and eyes dancing.

"Now, you all congratulate this young woman!" Ruth commanded. "She's an A number one heroine." Ruth offered Sara her arm, and they made their way out into the hall, moving rather slowly. Ruth led the way, right into the men's ward.

"Well, he *was* here!" Ruth said, indicating an empty bed.

Sara managed not to scream, but the terror in her face must have been obvious. The old woman hugged her. "You just hold your horses, child. I'm sure he's right as rain. What you need is your pretty robe and sexy night-gown—"

A wheelchair rumbled into the ward, and Sara let go of her short, gaping gown, rushing to touch Niall.

"Are you all right?" she demanded, practically in his lap.

"Thanks to you—yes, Sara," he said. "My little champ! You landed that plane! You're fantastic!"

"I know that. Tell me about you."

"Cranial films showed no concussion. It's a peculiarly wrenched neck. Put me into syncope, and the oxygen pressure at nine thousand feet sure wouldn't help keep me conscious. Scared me, just now, when I caught a ride in to see you still sleeping. Any pain?" Grasping her by both arms, he squinted at her bandages.

"Not a twinge. They must've filled me up with codeine. How long was I out?"

"You two sound," interrupted Ruth, "like a pair of quacks at a surgeons' conference. Get back to bed, Niall. I'm paying for repairs on you youngsters, so take advantage of all that this repair shop offers."

"Put Sara back to bed, Ruth," said Niall. "I owe her my life."

Retrieving her hands from Niall's, Sara began her retreat. The stout hospital matron half carried her back to bed, saying, "We've missed having you and your salmon serum in our kitchen, Sara. A pity you've come back to us as a patient."

"What time is it?" asked Sara. "I hope it's still Sunday."

"That it is. Nearly five." said Ruth. "You get some rest now."

Sara slept dreamlessly, and in the morning was eager for her release. Ruth came in right after breakfast.

"My kids can go home now," she told the chief surgeon.

"I'd prefer to keep them here, today, Ruth, but it's all right if you'll take the responsibility for them."

Niall was walking with a livelier step than Sara's when he signed himself out of the hospital.

Not surprisingly, Duncan Karnes couldn't avoid seeing them before their release. Toying with the stethoscope dangling from the pocket of his white coat, he glared sideways at Niall.

"Almost got yourself killed, I hear, Whitethorne. And you almost took Sara with you—one shard of glass just missed her jugular. I'd think you'd never want to show your face in this valley again."

Niall totally ignored him. Sara had parted her lips to spit out a furious retort, when Ruth Bell practically leaped between the two men.

"Do you realize to whom you are speaking?" she demanded of Duncan.

"Mrs. Bell! Nice to see you again—"

"I mean *him*!" She pointed abruptly at Niall. "Him. The gentleman you called Whitethorne."

Duncan found the nerve to retort, "I've called the chap worse things than that!"

"Well, chap, you'd better learn to call Dr. Whitethorne by his title."

"Doctor?" Duncan's exclamation sounded so strangled that Sara almost felt sorry for him.

Ruth had barely begun her tirade. "This gentleman who so kindly took pity on my roof and then agreed to shoot bears for Sara, happens to be—please note," she announced with maddening thoroughness, "a doctor of veterinary medicine. A veterinary surgeon."

She stepped closer to Duncan, looking almost straight up into his flaming face.

"And *that*, in my book, *Dr.* Karnes, is pretty nearly equivalent to *your* vaunted degree."

Niall was having a hard time keeping a straight face as he shoved Ruth through the nearest door, half carrying

Sara. The three of them managed to get out of the hospital and down to the dock before Sara's composure burst.

"Ruth, I loved it. Poor Duncan! So Niall relented and told you his profession?"

"I dragged it out of him last night, after he showed he could speak doctor-talk. I've been suspicious of Niall for weeks."

"So have I," Sara said, smiling.

When they were all crammed into the float plane Ruth had commandeered, the woman announced, "Myself, I'm headed back to Bumbry, 'cause the festivities aren't yet ended. Our pilot, Mr. Ransome, here, will drop you off at Green Lodge. You kids take it easy. I didn't get you out of the hospital to have either of you relapsing."

"We'll be at Green Lodge alone?" asked Sara. "Bettina isn't—"

"She's up to Bumbry, frolicking."

To Sara's relief Ruth didn't make any salacious comment as she bid farewell to them from the plane window.

"Until my plane's repaired, you're stuck here. Enjoy a day of rest, children."

Sara didn't mention that she was perfectly capable of walking the half mile to the stream to finish her salmon sampling. Once the plane was out of sight, she'd get back to work. There were only five more days before her departure, and her project must be finished by then.

"Okay, Sara," said Niall, towering over her. "You heard the boss. You've been shaken up and injured. Let's take a rest today."

"You rest. You're the only one really injured. I have a date with a few dozen of my favorite salmon."

"Not on your own, you won't go down there!"

"I can carry your rifle. Dad taught me to shoot when I was just a kid."

"You can't stick salmon and shoot at the same time,

171

and an injured grizzly is twice as dangerous as a healthy one."

"We'll see," Sara said, using her mother's phrase to postpone decisions until a man's mood can be altered. "It's hardly ten thirty, and it's going to be another gorgeous day today."

Both of them avoided mentioning Sara's inevitable departure in just five days. Kentucky seemed like another world to her now, and, strangely, it didn't feel like home anymore. This valley felt like home. Looking up at Niall's sculptured features as he gazed out at the snowy mountains, she knew he felt the same way.

If one cannot remain in paradise, she told herself, it's better not to experience paradise at all.

Then she jerked her thoughts back to the present.

"Look, Niall, you know I'm able to handle the fish by myself at this stage. They're totally shot; they haven't energy left to fight. And we haven't seen a single bear since the one that ate our garbage that night."

"And the one with cubs that looked in on us four days ago when you didn't even notice."

"What bear? I'd sure have heard you fire that cannon-size rifle."

"I didn't."

"Why not?"

He shrugged. "They saw me and fled. Why throw my weight around? They've got more right to fish for salmon than we have."

Sara smiled. This was the Niall she most loved, the kind-hearted veterinarian. There was also that half-tipsy bronc rider who risked his neck saving a life. She slid her hand into his.

"Sara," he said, "remember the evening you first saw Green Lodge? When you were so weary you hardly could walk?"

"And you had to help me undress for my bath?" she added, remembering very clearly.

"Come on," he said, low in his throat. "Come in the house, and let's finish that scene as it ought to have ended."

"But it's mid-morning! I've already—"

"Hospital baths are a nuisance," he said. "One cannot bathe properly in bed with a basin!"

"That sounds like something Duncan would say," she teased him. "Not my handsome hunk of a cowboy."

"You wait and see if I'm Duncan or not," he said, grabbing her. "Just you wait, lassie!"

She didn't have to wait long.

Upstairs in the coziest of bathing rooms, Niall sat her down on the dressing-table stool, then began to fill the deep tub. He dumped in some bubble bath too. At least it wasn't jasmine-scented this time. The room filled instead with the fragrance of lilacs.

"Oh, no," he said, seeing her bending forward. "You can't get your own boots off, remember?"

She remembered. She certainly—vividly—remembered.

Gazing at her as if she were the most precious being on earth, Niall knelt on one knee, just as he'd done that first night, and pulled off her boots, one after the other. Then he reached for Sara.

"Niall, may I say it again—on home ground? I love you."

Slowly and carefully, he drew her rumpled cowgirl shirt down her arms, and laid his face in the valley between her breasts. "Sara," his voice said, breath warm against her flesh. "I *adore* you."

Then he quickly shed his own shirt.

In the same sheepskin-carpeted, sweet-scented room where she began her sojourn at Green Lodge, rainbows of bubbles were rising in the long, high-sided tub. She again

173

felt weary—as Ruth might say, "besotted with love." The man she loved knelt before her, like an old-fashioned gentleman preparing to propose.

His hands gently cupped her breasts, freed now from the clinging bra. He kissed one, then the other, his tongue teasing the tips. She arched her back toward him as he took each one into his mouth.

"Marry me, Sara," he breathed against her flushed skin.

"I can't," she whispered, her voice already breaking. "Niall, I can't! How could we ever see each other? With me back in Kentucky and you, in Alberta or Saskatchewan—"

"Then we'll enjoy what we once wished very much to enjoy, Sara," he said bleakly, and began to unbuckle her belt.

She let him. She sniffed back tears and gave herself up to sweet rapture.

There was no icy-cold washcloth this time on her throat, but warm kisses. His big hands slid down her back, massaging it.

"Such a delicate back," he murmured. "Like a little bird's, but surprisingly strong."

She did what she'd once wanted to do—wonderingly touched his slim, straight nose, and like a blind girl read his features with stroking fingertips. The jut of his cheekbones, the caves where his eyes dwelt, the smooth, freshly shaven jaws. His lips captured her fingertips, nibbling them, causing her pulses to throb from her temples down to her hips.

"Niall . . ."

"My Sara, I'll have you this time, you know. There's no escaping it. No one in the house now except you and me."

"Thank goodness."

Smiling, he rose to take off his boots and jeans, and she watched him, struck by the junction where muscular

174

thighs narrowed to fit the slim pelvis. His hips were all of muscle, no padding at all.

He bent over Sara again, lifted her up off her feet, against him, and pulled down her jeans.

Then a warm, strong hand slid under her knees. Before she could caution this man who had had a Brahma half crush him and had survived a plane crash in one day, he picked her up and carried her to the bathtub.

"In you go, lovely," he said.

And in he came, after her.

They sat facing each other in the hot, chest-deep water. They were festooned with popping bubbles. He drew her legs over his, grasping her about the waist to slide her closer, closer, so she could loop both arms about his neck. Her slick, shining breasts bobbed against his bare chest as he tilted her toward him. Their lips met, first lightly, tenderly. Then he steadied her head and possessed her mouth, sitting gradually forward, tilting her backward as her thighs tightened around his slender waist.

"Now," he murmured into her open mouth. From the foamy depths he rose up . . . and in . . .

She groaned, feeling him, drawing him into her as she lay back in the water in his arms. Niall's face was pushed between her breasts so deeply she feared he might smother. She didn't feel a bit short of blood or of energy as she moved in rhythm with him and swirled round and round, making waves.

Streaming bubbles, they convulsed in sheer pleasure, splashing the white sheepskin rug, crying out in joy.

CHAPTER SEVENTEEN

Niall barely made it to his bedroom with her before he collapsed. They fell laughing on his bed—nude, pink from the steam, and still slightly damp.

"We've gotten your sticking-plaster a bit wet, Sara," he said, examining the small pad on the side of her neck.

"Will you examine me, Doctor, if I make the appropriate responses?" she said merrily.

"Your responses are just wonderful," he murmured, holding her tight as she lay beside him on the high bed.

"I mean appropriate for a veterinarian," she said, and gave two soft, short barks: "Arf, arf."

They both shook with laughter.

"Then, my precious pup—No, I'll call you my cuddlesome kitten—I shall have to prescribe treatment."

"What kind?"

"Oh, I think one more dose . . ."

Finally exhausted, he fell over on his side without opening his eyes. She hoped he would sleep.

Sara eased herself very slowly off the bed, and folded half the quilt up over her lover's naked body.

"Sleep, darling," she said softly.

She went straight to her bedroom, got into fresh jeans and a green workshirt, found her boots in the bathroom, pulled the plug in the tub, and—carrying her boots—ran right downstairs.

In the kitchen, racks of capped test tubes awaited her, row upon row of them, ready to be labeled with the number of each salmon met again and again in the streams. Poor salmon. Their lives were not their own. No privacy at all for their lovemaking.

Sara felt fresh, energetic, and also determined.

First, she stowed scores of test tubes in her backpack, along with syringes. No need for TMS anesthetic or for spaghetti tags, since salmon up here on the mountain were weak enough to cooperate and already wore tags from their previous encounters.

There wasn't much to carry. She was strong enough to lug her supplies and also to bring Niall's rifle along, though she had to pull up a chair to stand on in order to reach the big thing on the wall.

It was already loaded.

She wished he'd shown her how to handle it. This was like flying the airplane all over again, she thought ruefully, but she'd never felt more compelled to act.

She might be his beloved, but she wasn't merely Niall's cuddlesome kitten. That phrase was okay in bed, but her life didn't begin and end in the bedroom. Or the kitchen or nursery.

She'd had her fun. Now the work must be completed. She must catch her tagged salmon at the end of their run, for theirs would be the most interesting serum of all. In them, thyroid exhaustion would be almost complete. TRF —thyrotropin releasing factor—would be rushing from each salmon's hypothalamus to its pituitary gland, which in turn would try to stimulate more thyroxine production.

There'd be a publishable article from this—with a tongue-twister title like "Blood Concentration of Thyroxin in Reproductively Mature Salmon." She'd submit it to the *Transactions of the American Fisheries Society* or the Canadian *Journal of Fisheries*. Her gerontology institute, of course, would try to apply her findings to aging human beings. She'd apply for another summer grant.

That's where all the money went—to research on human health. People forget that most breakthroughs in medicine spring from fortunate accidents or from basic research done with no specific aim in mind.

Thinking these thoughts, she slung Niall's big-game rifle over her shoulder, barrel pointing up; she wasn't about to shoot herself in the foot.

Donning her backpack, she slipped out of Green Lodge and headed at a fast trot down the path to the highest-altitude salmon stream.

It was noon now, the least likely time for animals to seek food. A hundred to one she'd see no moose, no deer, not even a bird. Not to mention a bear. It was so hot that animals sought shade for their siestas. If she got a half day's work done today, she'd be sure to complete the project in time.

Work also would take her mind off Niall or at least distract her a little from their insoluble problems.

Warm sunshine turned softly fluttering leaves to green-gold coins. Pink and white wildflowers edged her path, and between tall trunks she caught a glimpse of the snowy glacier at the head of the valley, melting endlessly into the river.

Soon she'd fly over that glacier again, flying away from Niall. But, she mustn't think about that. She wasn't even eager to climb into an airplane again after her frightening landing. It would be like getting back on a horse after a fall. Niall would probably be leery of Brahma bulls, too, from now on. She smiled as she thought of him sleeping peacefully, then forced herself to get back to work.

Just as she expected, her poor salmon, exhausted by their long swim upstream and depleted by spawning, were easy to grab. She took off her boots to wade barefoot in the shallows. Here, no broken glass bottles threatened her feet, and no trash littered the shore. There was no sign, here, of anyone else. This area was wilderness, free even of hunters and loggers.

She did her sampling by pinning each fish under her left arm, across her thigh, half kneeling in the water to do so. She got soaked, but the sun dried her, and the breeze was gentle.

Her tagged salmon were everywhere, trailing their colorful little banners. She might have named them instead of numbered them: "Jake" instead of "84," "Melissa," instead of "106."

She straightened up after each salmon was caught and released, and carefully turned around 360 degrees, scanning the forested shores.

She was really more efficient alone than with Niall present. She'd looked at him too often, talked with him too much. Of course, he encouraged them all to make noises, shouting to each other over the water music. Bears, being hard of hearing, need plenty of warning that this spot is taken.

Sara began singing Broadway show tunes.

She didn't make herself check her watch until four twenty, amazed at how long she'd been at it. She arched her back and did a few upper-body calisthenics to free up her vertebrae. The sun was headed for the western mountain ridge, though it still had a good distance to go.

Her test tubes were almost gone. She should have

brought half again as many. "Good Sara," she praised herself, as if talking to her parents' dog. "You did good today, Sara. Won't Niall be impressed?"

Niall, she feared, would express a lot more than pleased astonishment.

Ten salmon later, it was nearly five forty, and the evening breeze began to chill her drenched torso. Time to close up shop, she thought.

She carried her test-tube racks to shore, filled her backpack with discarded syringes and the precious capped and labeled tubes, and took a last look at the circling, lolling, now-ancient salmon in the water below her. At least they wouldn't die in vain. Science would benefit from their involuntary donations to her project.

"Thanks guys and gals," Sara whispered, glad no one was around to call her sentimental. If she didn't have to live in a tiny apartment, she'd own six dogs and cats, and maybe a pair of Coho salmon in the bathtub. *No. Don't be silly, Sara—you're punchy from exhaustion.*

She grinned at her foolishness, looked up- and downstream, and then her grin lost its brightness. It froze into place.

He was tall, dark, and handsome—to any female of his own species—but not to her. Sara's limbs would not move. She stared at him the way he stared at her . . . from not very far away.

A grizzly bear, in the flesh. Walking toward her, coming down to fish for salmon.

A gigantic, hump-backed, silver-tipped grizzly.

Niall turned over and rubbed his eyes. What room was this? In hospital? No, not with log walls. He threw back the quilt from over him. Sara? No Sara. He squinted at the window. Low sun. Maybe five o'clock. Six.

"Sara?" He sat up. "Sara? Where are you, Sara?"

180

Then he fell back on the mattress, aching all over. He knew exactly where Sara must be. She was replaying their first days together exactly as events had happened. First the amorous bath, then the tumble in bed, and this was the time of evening when he and Ruth had once fooled Sara—brought her that comical breakfast in bed.

Any minute Sara would come through that door, lugging a tray. She'd be laughing and teasing, and they'd share a meal together. He was famished.

He'd give her a little more time in the kitchen. No fragrance of frying bacon had wafted upstairs, though the bedroom door stood ajar. He didn't want to drop off to sleep again though. Amazing, that he'd slept since noon. How long had Sara herself slept?

Sara MacFarland deserved to be adored. While hanging upside down in the airplane, so the doctors told him, she kept screaming for people to help him. He marveled at such unselfish courage. She'd fought like a tigress to save him. *That's love.*

That's unbelievable love. He wondered if he deserved it.

He thought of Sara comforting him in the rodeo ring, Sara kissing his bruised body and saying he was idiotic to try to fly home in the plane. He now had to admit she was right.

He wished he could risk his life once for Sara, just to even things out a little.

She didn't come feed him, so he got out of bed, put on some pants, and dug a clean shirt out of the wardrobe. He went downstairs, hearing nothing, seeing nothing, and smelling nothing cooking.

In the kitchen there seemed to be some test-tube racks missing.

In the front room there seemed to be a blank space up on the wall where previously hung—

"Oh my God, Sara!" he shouted.

181

The big-game rifle was gone.

Sara gazed at the grizzly. The grizzly solemnly contemplated Sara. The rifle was out of reach, and any fast motion she might make would be insane.

She remembered what Niall had said she must do. Lie down and cover her head with her arms. Firmly, she commanded both knees to bend. Like a small supplicant, still facing the bear that stood a dozen feet away, she knelt down.

"Please, bear. Please . . ."

Then she very slowly lay facedown on the pebbly shore, and crossed both arms up over her head.

She didn't have long to wait. And pray.

The bear approached. She could hear the stones crunching; hear its wheezing. Then she could smell it as well. Her eyes squeezed tightly shut, she refused to see anything, even the stones beneath her nose.

The nose of the grizzly moved over her back. Over her head. It exhaled in her ear, ruffling her curls. She ceased breathing at all. *Please, bear.*

Something spiky touched her back. Tentatively, it stroked her wet shirt, and then stroked her again. In her mind's eye Sara saw a cat. With one paw, it softly stroked a mouse, examining it. Deciding what to do with it.

And this was no tabby cat. This was a half-ton bear.

Again she wished she would faint—miss this scene altogether, the way Niall had missed their plane crash.

Why did the grizzly take so long to decide what to do to her?

She distinctly heard and felt the bear sigh. She even smelled its fishy breath. Then rocks rattled nearby, and then farther away. She listened to splashing. Millimeter by millimeter she lifted her head and peeked out.

A fish flew up out of the water and hit her in the ribs,

bouncing onto the pebbled shore. It flapped once and lay still. The grizzly strolled up the shore, retrieved his fish, and gulped it down. Then he went wading again. Fishing.

Sara couldn't help imagining that he must be a semi-vegetarian. He'd eat fish, but not red meat. She couldn't control herself any longer. Hysterically, she giggled. The grizzly turned his head and looked at her, a salmon hanging out of his mouth like a silver cigar.

Then he slapped the water and sent another fish sailing through the air.

She wouldn't be chewed up and eaten. She'd be buried alive for her sins—in slimy, wet salmon! She giggled until tears filled her eyes.

The bear moved a little bit downstream, showing her his broad rump. Suddenly he let out the biggest belch she'd ever heard. Sara, both hands over her mouth, lying face-down, limp as a beached salmon, burst into laughter.

The next rattle of rocks brought her head up sharply. More grizzlies? This bear's wife and children?

Up on her knees, she screamed.

"No, Niall!"

He'd run across her field of vision as he dove for the rifle.

"Don't you shoot him! He's my bear!"

"Sara!" Niall shouted. "Get out of the way!"

She spun around, to see her grizzly wading hastily downstream, looking back over his shoulder.

"He's leaving! He's harmless! Don't shoot him!"

She ran to Niall and grabbed the barrel of the gun, wrenching it upward. He jerked it out of her grasp and raised it like a club, his face livid with fury.

"You crazy little idiot! Damn you to hell, Sara!"

"Well, I—" she panted, anger building within her.

He grabbed for her arm and whirled her around behind him, out of his way.

183

"Don't you shoot my bear, you murderer!"

"Murderer! You were inches from death, you bloody idiot! I oughta kill you, not the bear!" He was stammering, the whites of his eyes showing, and his whole body shook.

"Don't you talk to me like that, Niall. I had work to do! I couldn't just . . ."

The rifle swinging in his right hand, Niall swooped down on her backpack, threw it over one shoulder, and caught Sara by the elbow, forcing her into the trees.

"I'm gonna sling this damned pack over a cliff!" he fumed. "It's not worth your life! You crazy woman! I can't believe I stood there and watched a huge grizzly poke you. I didn't dare do a thing. And you laughed. You lay there and giggled. I've never seen anything more stupid in my life! And for what! Some damn experiment!"

"I was laughing from relief. And that damn experiment is very important to me!" She couldn't believe this was happening—just hours ago they were making beautiful love and now she could have cheerfully killed him.

"I could wring your neck, Sara!"

Even now they were on the same wavelength.

"Go on, try it. Big rodeo star who almost gets us both killed in an airplane. How dare you act so superior!"

"I'm not acting superior. I admit I made a bad judgment. Like you did today. I said *never* go to the streams unprotected!"

"I didn't need you along!" she screamed. "I can do my work alone."

"Like some little toddler: 'Look, Mom, I can do it all by myself.' What're you trying to prove, Sara? That you can walk on water? The biggest man alive shouldn't work in the streams this season solo. I am not standing by and watching you get yourself killed."

"A bear's different from a bronco or a bull, huh? Big

shot! At least I take chances for a damned good reason, not just to show off! And not with someone else along!"

"I went into that chute with that bull to save a man's life," he told her.

She turned away from him, then turned back again. She didn't recognize this angry, hostile man.

"Hand me my pack. Right now. Hand it over." Her voice was cold.

He jerked it off his shoulder and thrust it at her.

Sara stuck her arms through the straps and lugged her collection of samples up the path to the lodge, ignoring the tall man behind her. Damn him! How dare he treat her like a child. Belittle her work! He was just like all the rest.

All the way back she told herself to hate him, and she went up to her room without supper, still trembling with fury. Okay. Maybe it was the best thing in the world. It's over. Fall in love and fall right back out again.

CHAPTER EIGHTEEN

The next evening Ruth Bell came home.

"And how are the lovers enjoying their lovely taste of privacy?" was her opening sally. "Peace and quiet around here for once, without my nattering and Bettina's nagging."

Just as after their quarrel in the lake, Sara and Niall automatically pretended nothing was amiss. However, their charade couldn't for one moment fool Ruth.

"Oh, oh!" she said, "I sense a bit of a fracas."

"Sara enjoys being caressed by a grizzly," said Niall.

"You actually sound jealous," Sara said grumpily.

"You're not telling me," Ruth began, "that Sara had grizzly problems?"

"Exactly that," Niall said. "She slipped off to work alone in the stream, and was almost killed."

"I was not! He never hurt me one bit! He only threw fish at me and belched."

Instead of being furious, this time Sara suddenly felt like laughing. But she couldn't give in now. She had to make

Ruth understand. This was serious. "I won't be treated like a baby. Or an idiot."

Niall said, "Then don't act like one."

"I wouldn't yell at you!" she stormed, though she'd lost the momentum of her anger. "Call you a bloody idiot that I'd like to murder!"

"I'll wager a hundred dollars that you called me worse than that recently, and threatened to murder me too. Very recently, Sara MacFarland!"

"When?" she demanded.

"When I passed out in the air, and you had to land that blasted airplane!"

"Children, don't squabble; you'll make me cross with you," Ruth said. "Just imagine! Dr. Whitethorne and our soon-to-be Dr. MacFarland are squabbling like infants."

"I just try to ensure that she does become Dr. MacFarland, not Dead-Woman MacFarland."

"Would you two please kiss and make up?" Ruth suggested.

Sara glared over at Niall. He glared back.

All at once Sara couldn't take it anymore. It *was* serious, but it was also so . . . ridiculous. She burst out in bubbling laughter.

Niall cried, "This little . . . daredevil's sense of humor is . . . is . . . absurd!"

But a grin cracked the granite of his features.

"Now, that's better, children," said Ruth.

"Come here, Sara," said Niall. "I didn't hit you, remember? I only wanted to—to paddle your bottom. I apologize. I insulted your dignity. Here, have a go at me instead." He dropped his defenses and waited.

"Oh, Niall . . ."

"I still love you," he said, as if Ruth were not there listening.

Sara held out for two more minutes, frowning and

searching for a retort. Then she began to see what had happened. Not to her, but to Niall.

"Maybe you had some right to be angry, Niall. Over the bear. But you also were furious because you didn't get to save my life."

"I wouldn't put it—"

"Just hear me out, Niall. You did save my life. Another bear might've come along. When you got hold of the rifle, I did suddenly feel safe. Safe enough to get furious with you."

"I'm sorry I yelled at you. C'mere, Sara."

She went. She put her arms around Niall's waist and rested her head on his chest.

Ruth grinned. "That's more like it. Nasty, quarrelsome children don't get any presents. They get sent straight up to bed." She lifted one eyebrow. "Maybe that wouldn't seem like punishment to you two, but I think a little present might stir interest, as well."

Both of them cocked their heads, unsure what to say.

"Sit down. Don't want you falling down. Plane crash, bulls, bears—whatever will you get tangled up in next? Now tell me: when's the wedding?"

Recovering from the jolt of that question, Sara said, "There won't be one."

It was Niall's turn to give a jerk, as if she'd run a knife into him.

"We can't think about marriage. We realize that," she explained. "Look where I work, and who knows where Niall will next have to settle down."

"Settle down here, both of you."

Niall answered for both of them, "Thank you very much, Ruth, but only on holiday could we ever—"

"Now, just hold your horses, lad. I'm not finished. Do you realize what a burden a gigantic old fort like this can be? I can't pilot a plane, so I'm at the mercy of whoever deigns to fly me up this mountain. Suppose I fell ill; I could perish. I want to move down to the valley."

"I hope you don't plan to sell to a timber company," said Niall.

"Log this land? These sheer slopes? Insanity! You told me that yourself. Without trees all the soil would slide down into the river. Turn it muddy. Silt it up. No more salmon."

Sara glanced over at Niall. His eyes were riveted on Ruth.

"So what I am going to do—and my mind's made up, children—what I am already arranging to do—I've been making telephone calls from Bumbry already—is to make a present of this house and this land."

"Oh, no. Not to—" Sara began.

"Not to you, child. I'm not quite *that* foolish. It wouldn't do the two of you much good to own this place. You'd have to sell it off. Not even a decent location for a veterinary clinic."

"Niall doesn't do that sort of vet work—"

"I know what kind of work he wants to do. He's talked my ear off about playing doctor to wildlife. Well, I've begun a little chat with the Canadian Wildlife Federation. Whetting their appetite. They don't get a chunk of untouched wilderness handed to them every day, not with a building on it quite large enough to become a research station."

"Oh, Ruth!" gasped Sara, gripping Niall's hand.

"And what do you have to say, Dr. Whitethorne?"

"I can't believe what I'm hearing."

"You reckoned I was a stingy old skinflint? A mean old miser? You don't even know that I looked into your past, my boy, and found out you used to live here. Grew up right here in Green Lodge and never told me."

"Whenever did you find that out?" he asked.

"After you said you were a vet. I asked around. At first I wondered if you came back here for revenge. Mr. Bell had caused your folks to lose their home and jobs, I remember. He never listened to me. Then it looked like you came back just for nostalgia's sake. That's nice. I like a man with a heart."

Niall was speechless.

"Now I come to the best part," Ruth continued. "If I give 'em my land—and I can afford to, rest assured—then I get some say in what the wildlife folks do with it, see? Even in the event of my death—which I don't plan on for at least fifteen years—this'll be a station for wildlife biology. Grizzlies and salmon and such."

Sara shook her head in amazement. Niall was still paralyzed.

"You can do that?" Sara asked. "Specify?"

"Sure I can. They say I can. I pay for it, I call the shots."

"But—"

"Stop throwing cold water on my project!" cried Ruth. "I never threw cold water on yours! Now, listen to me. You get yourself right back to Kentucky, Sara, and finish up that degree. Fish physil-ology, or whatever. Niall's got all his training—in just the right things. He'll work here, or they don't get a penny. . . .

"I work here?"

"Certainly not as boss, not yet." She waggled a finger at Niall. "You'll have to work your way up to the top, lad. But you can live here, where you work. The two of you can. I've got no children. I want to leave some young people happy."

"I can't believe this!" cried Sara. "Please, nobody wake me up. I don't want to find out it's a dream!"

"You two see why I got cross with you? Walking in, just

190

dying to tell you my surprise, and I find you squabbling. Over a ruddy belching bear!"

Sara whooped with laughter and flung her arms around Ruth so tightly that the tiny woman grunted. "I love you, Ruth."

"Let's not break the philanthropist," Ruth said, struggling. "Did I tell you my land will be a wildlife preserve in perpetuity?"

"That's incredibly generous," said Niall, moving Sara out of his path so he could get his own arms around Ruth.

"Hey! Don't you squash me. Get on with you, Niall! Go hug your fiancée. I presume that's what she is by now. Enough living in sin. You two get married! By this time next year, understand?"

Sara and Niall nodded emphatically, arms about each other. Right in front of Ruth, they kissed.

"Just one more thing," Ruth said, shaking an impressively gnarled finger at Niall. "Don't you ever pull a trick like that again on me. And on dear little Sara MacFarland. Made fools of us both, you did."

"I did? When?"

"Yes, you did. It was you under that mask, not Elmer Snagg."

"The rain dance," cried Sara, nudging Niall in the ribs. "She's even dug out the truth about the rain dance!"

"We are not going to have *any* privacy," said Niall, grinning from ear to ear.

Sara responded, "A small price to pay, to live together. And to live here in paradise."

"With no more secrets left," Niall told her. "I think we've finally run out of revelations."

"Yes." She hugged him. "No more secrets. All of our secrets are shared."